BadDay inBlackrock

KevinPower

The Lilliput Press
Dublin

First published 2008 by
THE LILLIPUT PRESS
62–63 Sitric Road, Arbour Hill
Dublin 7, Ireland
www.lilliputpress.ie

ISBN 978 1 84351 146 5

3 5 7 9 10 8 6 4 2

A CIP record for this title is available
from The British Library.

Set in 10.5 pt on 13.5 pt Minion by Marsha Swan
Printed in Ireland by ColourBooks, Dublin

ACKNOWLEDGMENTS

Some thanks are due:

To Frank McGuinness, for his support, guidance and unfailing kindness; to Antony Farrell and all at The Lilliput Press, particularly Fiona Dunne, Kathy Gilfillan, Vivienne Guinness and Elske Rahill, for their enthusiasm and attention to detail; to Lucy Luck, for generous help and advice; to Ron Callan, for his faultless stewardship of my PhD; to Marie Butterly, for support moral, financial and intellectual; and to some invaluable early readers: Jeanne-Marie Ryan, Simon Ashe-Browne, Dave Fleming, Eoin O'Connell, Jesse Weaver, Faela Stafford, Louise Aitchison, Adam Kelly and Amy Dwyer.

AUTHOR'S NOTE

This novel is a work of the imagination. While certain aspects of the narrative have been inspired by news coverage of actual events, all of the characters – their actions and experiences, their histories and destinies – are fictional, and are not intended to represent actual persons, living or dead. The same applies to the educational, medical, social and legal institutions that appear in the text.

This is th'impostume of much wealth and peace,
That inward breaks, and shows no cause without
Why the man dies.

Hamlet, IV:4

PART ONE

Facts and Values

1

They came to the big white house on Inishfall. This much is true, this much we know for sure.

When the last of the trials was over, Richard Culhane's parents packed up and sold their house in Dublin. They went to live for an indefinite period in their windswept house on Inishfall, an island off the coast of Kerry where the Culhanes had holidayed every summer for the first twelve years of Richard's life. I've never been to Inishfall, but I have seen a picture of the house the Culhanes keep there – it was printed in two or three of the newspapers when the story as a whole was winding down. It's a weatherbeaten two-storey manor, painted white, though the paint is turning grey and psoriatic in the rain blown in from the sea. The house looks as though it should be surrounded by the ruins of a vast estate. This is proper, I suppose. It has become the final refuge of a fallen family.

I haven't seen the Culhanes in several months. I was there, outside the Dublin courthouse, when the last of the verdicts came through and the family attempted to leave. For two or three minutes – a frozen moment, it might have been a dozen times that long – the Culhanes were marooned on the steps of the courthouse, their exit barred by the ranks of journalists and television cameras. Peter Culhane stood with his arm around his wife, holding her so tightly he might have been posing for a joke photograph – *See? It's scary how much I love my wife!* – but he didn't smile. Eventually the bailiff shouldered a path through the crowd, and the family, with Richard in the lead, a sports jacket pulled up over his head, managed to reach their car.

That was the last time I saw the Culhanes. But I often think of them out there in the west, safe in their big white house on Inishfall. How do they spend their days? What do they talk about? What does Richard say to his mother when he runs into her in the kitchen, late at night? Do they talk about injustice? Do they talk about money and power? Do they talk about death?

There is no way of knowing these things. We are, each of us, alone with our guesses. I've never heard anyone talk about this: about what life must be like for the Culhanes on Inishfall. Safer just to leave them be, we tell each other. Best to let them get on with their lives. What this means, of course, is that *we* want to be left alone, *we* want to get on with *our* lives, however ravaged and empty they may be. The Culhanes, and everything that happened to them, have taken up too much of our thoughts already. They have haunted us enough, these usurpers of our time, our love.

I'd like to pay a visit, some time soon, to Inishfall, not to talk to the Culhanes but simply to see the big white house first-hand, to listen to the sea and smell the rotting fish from the crab-traps and rockpools on the nearby beach. I think it might teach me something. I think it might offer me some answers to the questions I've been asking.

Our knowledge of events – even of those events that affect us most intimately – is partial. We content ourselves with guesswork. And that is what I have had to do, in composing this account: content myself with guesswork.

Although I knew most of the other people involved in the incident more or less well, I hardly knew Richard Culhane. We were at university together, but our classes were huge – over four hundred people – and until the events of this story, I knew him mostly by reputation. Richard seldom attended lectures but you could see him often, alone on the playing fields at evening, redfaced and stocky, practising his kicks. He seemed mysterious to me then and he seems mysterious to me now. During the trials he was the only one who kept silent, who sat with his back straight, facing the wall a few feet in front of him, and who never moved, never stood to offer an apology, never broke down and confessed. I think a visit to the big white house might teach me something about his stoicism, about his calm in the midst of collapse. Then again, I might learn nothing. I've become sanguine about the possibility of genuine knowledge. The world, when I consult it, returns only the hard glass of the mirror that is myself. I wonder if it is the same for Richard and his parents, if they ask the world for meaning only to be scorned, rebuffed; if they find themselves in the dark, as we do, still, now that everything is done.

2

I can't tell this story. Let's be clear about that from the beginning.

I wasn't there. I didn't see it happen. This is by way of an apology. I've had to piece it together, after the fact, from available sources, from newspapers, radio, television, magazines. And people spoke to me, too, usually in whispers, always in private, sometimes with a look of furtive shame, more often with a kind of half-concealed pity or sadness. Teachers and parents, interested parties, witnesses and friends: somehow they were always eager to talk, once I'd brought the subject up, once I'd declared an interest. In the hush of a southside living room, say, as afternoon wanes and turns to evening, at what Stephen O'Brien's popular parents always called the cocktail hour (as they tolerantly mixed the gin and tonics for some visiting college friends), people will often be amenable to sharing their memories of the night it happened, or the moment they heard it had happened, or their thoughts on what life must be like for the various families in the protracted and wearisome aftermath. They pay attention to their hands, as they talk. They seldom look at me.

You encounter resistance, too, of course. Many of my friends and acquaintances told me their parents had forbidden them to talk about the case. Recently I asked a girl I knew if she'd ever met the boy who died. 'We don't talk about that,' she said, looking alarmed.

I didn't press any further.

No, I wasn't there on the night itself. But I might have been. It might have happened to anyone, at any time, on any night. Nights out in Dublin have a sameness, a predictability. A pattern is followed, every time, without fail. Drinks in someone's house. A pub. A club. Kebabs or chips. A taxi home. But I don't want you to think of the central event of my story as something contingent, as a random occurrence, a freak of chance. You should remember that this event, one way or the other, was inevitable. It would have happened anyway, no matter what factors were different, no matter what people might have done differently.

Or so I've come to believe.

Violence is always an unspoken possibility on these nights out, despite our fondness for the pattern. We do a great deal of concealing, when we're on the town. We conceal our spots and our badly cut fringes, the T-shirt lines of our builder's tans. We conceal our anxieties, our insecurities. We conceal facts, too: facts about who we'd like to sleep with, who we'd like to kiss, who we fear and who we despise. And we conceal more disturbing things: a cigarette burn, self-inflicted; a scar from a razor blade, the same; a problem with food or drugs. But the most secret thing, the thing we go to the greatest lengths to hide, is the possibility of death, the possibility that one of us will go too far and not return, or that we will *all* go too far, that we will go too far because that's what everybody else is doing, because we'd be afraid to say no, afraid to hold back, afraid to ask the simple question – *Why?* Since Conor's death a lot of people have been asking *why* – in reading through those newspapers and magazines I come across it often, the anguished interrogative – but motives are something that happen afterward, they are what we read back into the inevitable. Motives are a way of finding sense where none was meant, where none was even looked for at the time.

Events of a certain magnitude barge their way into our shared future. But some events reach backwards in time, too, and make their contours felt years before they ever get around to actually happening. Conor Harris's death is one of these. We felt it coming, I think. Not that this did us much good. Not that it helped.

There is the fact of Conor's death. And there is the gallery of interpretations explaining why it happened. Facts and interpretations: these are what I have. These are all I have.

In several crucial ways, the case remains opaque. I dearly wish things had unfolded in some other, clearer way. But I am helplessly stuck with the recorded facts. Reality doesn't shape itself to meet the demands of art, and all storytelling is essentially a retrospective gesture. So I will follow the facts to their ends, to see what I find.

I've been afraid to tell this story, possibly because of what it reveals about the cannibalistic nature of my generation, about our hatred for each other, about our hatred for ourselves. I've been afraid to tell it because it seemed too dark, too unanswerable, too messily enigmatic to be told in simple terms. But I think I have to tell it, now. I am too alone in my fascination with it, too solitary in my fixation on the events of a few hours one night three years ago. Now that the trials are over, now that the papers have let the story grow cold, now that I have been left by myself, holding the frayed ends of all these facts, unable to tie them together in any way that satisfies me, I can try to talk about what happened. I no longer seem to have a choice.

This is a story about a single event and its consequences, about what happened before, and about how everything that happened afterward was different.

This is the worst thing that ever happened to us.

This is the only story I will ever be able to tell.

3

This is what happened.

On the last night of summer, 2004, at fifteen minutes past three in the morning, a twenty-year-old student was beaten and kicked to death outside Harry's Niteclub in Blackrock, County Dublin. Three other students were arrested just under a month later and eventually charged with manslaughter. The manslaughter charges didn't stick. Two of the boys were eventually tried in a Dublin court for violent disorder. They were found guilty and served five months in prison. The third boy, also convicted of violent disorder, served eleven months in prison. The state then attempted to bring the third boy to trial for manslaughter, but due to evidentiary difficulties the DPP was forced to enter a *nolle prosequi* and the case collapsed.

The student who died was named Conor Harris. I knew him.

The three students who went to prison for violent disorder were named Stephen O'Brien, Barry Fox and Richard Culhane.

For a brief period Stephen O'Brien and I were at the same private school together. Richard Culhane and Barry Fox went to a different private school. But, in the way of Dublin schools, we all knew each other, in this way or that.

We all went to the same university. That's how I gleaned what first-hand knowledge I have about these people and their lives.

There was also a girl. I'll get to her soon.

The state pathologist (since retired) noted in his report on the incident that it was likely that, as well as suffering numerous blows to the face and neck, Conor Harris received three kicks to the head that were the probable cause of his death, two hours later, in the emergency room of St Vincent's Hospital.

I'll keep coming back to this pathologist's report.

Three kicks. Bang. Bang. Bang. The bar is closed, the people tumbling out. A fight develops, somewhere on the fringes of the crowd, near the bus stop on the packed main road. Those three kicks, we can be sure, aren't the only blows thrown. But they're the ones that count. According to the pathologist's report – the controversial one, the report on which so much would come to depend – the first and second kicks could have been fatal in themselves. So the third kick has seemed, to some, like a sort of gratuity, what in New Orleans they call a *lagniappe*: an added fillip, an extra bang for your buck. To people less concerned with the facts, however, or to people less inclined towards forgiveness, the third kick has to have been the fatal one.

These were rugby kicks: great semicircular sweeps from the hip, with the foot angled out to lift the ball, the arms extended to keep balance.

Bang. Bang. Bang. One, two, three. A tidy progression from injury to unconsciousness to death. People seem to have found it difficult to conceive of something so irrevocable happening so quickly. They find it difficult to imagine that, with the first kick, Conor Harris was already dead. So many people prefer to imagine that the third kick was the one that did the damage.

This is because the third kick was thrown by Richard Culhane, who up until that point, according to some of the eyewitness reports, had barely been involved in the fight at all.

As Harry's Niteclub emptied and everyone staggered out into the street and began to wave for taxis, Conor Harris found Richard Culhane in the crowd. It was the last night of summer, the return to school and college was imminent, people had come back from their J1 visas (Conor Harris had spent the summer of the previous year in San Diego, Richard Culhane had been in Ocean City), so there must have been an air of tired, expectant festivity in the club and on the street. It was the end of the evening, people had paired off or been disappointed, couples were making out in shop doorways or clumsily fucking in alleys or laneways. You could hear the boom and shuffle of the ocean at night from beyond the ramparts of the seaside railway station.

And Conor Harris found Richard Culhane in the crowd. Although they had both been in the same small vicinity all evening, they hadn't seen each other until now. Was Conor, at this point, *looking* for Richard Culhane? Was Richard looking for Conor? It's possible. Any number of things are possible.

Richard would have had his arm around a girl. This is the girl I'll get to soon. She was wearing a hoodie, black but spangled with silver stars. Conor would have recognized this hoodie.

Conor would have said something to Richard about the girl. The two boys would have started shouting.

Richard's friends saw what was happening and muscled over. Among them, looming largest, were Barry Fox and Stephen O'Brien. It was the end of the night. Everyone was drunk.

It isn't clear who threw the first punch. Richard always denied it was him. It might even have been Conor. But the punch was thrown and very quickly Conor was on the ground. Only one witness reported seeing him fall. He was surrounded by six to ten people, and they were still hitting him as he fell.

Not all of these people were kicking. Eyewitnesses would later be able to positively identify only three attackers who were kicking as well as punching.

Bang. Bang. Bang.

Two hours later Conor Harris was dead. He never regained consciousness. The next day in college someone would tell me that Conor had woken up in the ambulance long enough to say his ex-girlfriend's name. But this can only be a rumour, the sort of romantic legend that surfaces and quickly dies in the aftermath of a terrible event. Whatever Conor was thinking about during those two unconscious hours, I very much doubt it was Laura. They'd been broken up for several months, after all. I don't think people have properly understood that.

4

'THREE MEN ARRESTED IN NIGHTCLUB DEATH CASE', said the headline in *The Irish Times*, but we didn't think of them as men, and I doubt they thought of themselves that way, either. They were boys: the memory of school was still fresh for them, they could still show up for college badly shaven or with spots ripening on their chins. When we saw their pictures in the paper, we were shocked, I think, by how young they looked, how guileless and weak. The papers used the digital photo from Richard's UCD student card, and he looked blurry and anonymous, like any number of Quinn School jocks, his eyes dark under the gelled and lacquered hair. They used Debs photos of Stephen O'Brien, Barry Fox and Conor Harris, cropped so that the girls beside them disappeared, except for a female arm in gilded fabric at the western edge of the frame. I still have these pictures, clipped from various papers and magazines. I line them up in front of me. Bizarrely, it looks like the boys are all on the way to the same party. Here is Barry Fox, his cheeks still carrying their reassuring cargo of puppy fat, his eyes trained on the middle distance. Of the three, only Barry doesn't smile. The others offer uniformly those irrelevant grins: neither genuine nor posed, but simply an aspect of having your photograph taken. Here is Stephen O'Brien, with his rakish haircut and massive shoulders, looking like a man who's always in trouble. And here is Conor Harris, with his tiny girlfriend's bare shoulder dwarfed by his huge loose-limbed frame. These photos, in their ubiquity, have achieved the status of documents of fate: the doom of their subjects seems written in their amateurish lack of focus, in the goonish smiles of the tuxedoed boys, in the grim familiarity of the pose and the backdrop. Here they stand in various suburban living rooms, the killers and their smiling victim. Oddly, the use of his student ID picture seems somehow to remove Richard Culhane from involvement in the photos' fateful narrative; lined up next to the other three, he appears to belong to a different story, to be alone in his solitary drama, the odd man out.

But I've made the mistake of calling him a man again.

They were boys.

Remember that.

5

In the summer of 2003 Richard Culhane's father had a small heated swimming pool installed in the long back garden of the Culhanes' house in Sandycove.

Richard was in Ocean City at the time, working as a bartender in a small yacht club on the seafront and sleeping with a sweet New Jersey girl named Megan, who kept promising to visit Richard in Dublin, maybe in September or October 'if that was cool'. Richard kept trying to dissuade Megan from this plan. Richard already had a girlfriend in Dublin. Her name was Claire Lawrence. She had been to school (I think she was a St Brigid's girl, one of the 'Virgins on the Rocks') with Stephen O'Brien's cousin Rachel. Richard had been going out with Claire, off and on, since the summer before sixth year, when they were both seventeen.

Before Richard left for America his parents had thrown a going-away party and invited some of his college friends and most of his friends from school. Claire drank half a bottle of Smirnoff and clung to Richard all night, weepy and possessive. Richard was soothing – it was an unexpected gift of his, that ease he had with women. He was secretly proud of his mastery of two languages, the language of jockish derision and the subtler language that women seemed to speak. He told Claire he would always love her. He promised he wouldn't cheat on her. He swore they would pick up where they left off in September.

As it happened Megan never did come to Dublin. But Richard

broke up with Claire anyway, three weeks after he got back. In some way the swimming pool seemed to convince him he had to do it.

Peter Culhane told Richard nothing about the pool. He wanted it to be a surprise. Peter picked Richard up at the airport and drove him back to the house. The Culhanes' house always smelled of lavender and furniture polish. To Richard this was the smell of home, unchanged after his three months' absence. It was raining and he was proudly conscious of his American tan. He dumped his bags in the kitchen, next to the island that contained the oven and the second sink, and walked as if in slow motion out through the patio doors to get a look at the pool.

'Fuck me,' he said. 'That's *deadly*.'

Later he would be ashamed of this moment of gauche astonishment. When he told his friends about the pool he was careful to be as offhand as possible, as though material success was nothing new to him. That was how you dealt with things like swimming pools, Richard thought: as though you'd seen it all before.

Richard began to mock his father for having bought the pool in the first place. 'Dunno what the old pair were thinking,' he would scoff. 'A fucking *swimming pool* in *Dublin*, like. For the *two days* of sunshine we get every year, you know? Fucking pass me my Ray-Bans, like.'

But this was just another way of disavowing the secure and confident joy of owning a swimming pool.

Privately Richard was glad that he had been absent during the pool's construction. He knew that Peter would have spent the summer nattering away to the builders about paintings and share prices, unaware of how ridiculous they found him, these men in their grubby tracksuits and golden jewellery, men who spoke a language of which Peter was serenely ignorant, a language of coarse competence and trenchant masculinity. But Richard was glad the pool was there, shimmering like molten lead under temperate skies in the long back yard.

He had known, the minute he saw the pool, that he would have to break up with Claire Lawrence. Why? Because she just wasn't classy enough. She didn't deserve a boyfriend with a pool. She would get pissed on half a bottle of vodka, and monopolize Richard's attention in a bedroom when he could have been downstairs drinking with the lads. Sometimes she would cut herself with a razor blade, which she kept in her handbag in a neatly folded scrap of paper torn from a glossy fashion magazine. She was an embarrassment. 'Always opening her mouth at the wrong fucking moment,' Richard confided to Barry Fox. 'And not so I could shove my cock in it, you know?'

Barry and Richard high-fived.

For the first two weeks after the builders got the water heater up and running, Peter Culhane went out on to the patio in his dressing gown every morning and had breakfast sitting by the pool. It was very cold, and eventually he had to stop.

6

Three people killed Conor Harris outside Harry's Niteclub on the last night of summer, 2004. Two of them were Brookfield boys. The other had gone to Brookfield College and then transferred to Merrion Academy. These things matter. These things make a difference.

Brookfield College, founded by the Jesuits in 1872, occupies a leafy enclave off Mount Merrion Avenue in Blackrock. Merrion Academy takes up most of a Georgian terrace in Milltown. They're both rugby schools, they're both single-sex, and they're both famous for the outstanding achievements of their students. 'The percentage of students from Brookfield who do not go on to some form of third level education', says one broadsheet, 'is negligible.' Brookfield and Merrion Academy annually swap places at the top of the Irish second-level league table for private schools.

According to the Brookfield website, the school buildings 'are situated in bucolic grounds, a short distance from Dublin'. In the 'About Us' section of the site, there is a paragraph about 'the importance of faith to the ethos of the school', the necessity of imparting to students an ethic of both fortitude and faith.

The Brookfield admission papers advise that priority will be given, in considerations for admittance, to the sons and brothers of former Brookfield students. 'Parents are also requested to contribute to the Building Fund' (I am quoting now from the Brookfield prospectus, a glossy publication done in faux-Celtic style). According to a 'Vision Statement' included in this prospectus, Brookfield College expects that its pupils, on graduating, will have been inculcated with 'ideals of excellence in all aspects of their lives – spiritual, moral, intellectual'. I don't know if Richard Culhane was familiar with these words, but Peter Culhane certainly was.

Conor Harris was an exception to the sons-and-brothers rule. He got into Brookfield because his parents could afford to make what was described as 'a substantial donation' to the school, for the planned refurbishment of the gymnasium. Figures for this donation have not been disclosed.

The school has a Latin motto: *Semper et Ubique Fidelis*.

It means 'Always and Everywhere Faithful'.

Two former presidents of the Irish Republic had gone to Brookfield. According to one report, 'It is harder to get into Brookfield than it is to get into Oxford.'

The school takes in a small number of boarders every year. Neither Richard Culhane nor Conor Harris, both of whom lived close enough to the school to be driven there every morning, belonged to this number.

Conor Harris's parents habitually drove him to school. During his last year at Brookfield Richard drove himself, in the Nissan Almera his parents had bought him for his seventeenth birthday.

The halls of Brookfield are lined with polished wooden lockers and framed pages from newspapers dating back to the turn of the century. These pages memorialize the school's sporting successes. You can't visit Brookfield without being made aware of how seriously the school take sports of all kinds, and rugby in particular.

At the beginning of their fifth year at Brookfield Richard Culhane and Barry Fox formed a band called the Paranoids. Richard was a passable rhythm guitarist but Barry, the vocalist, was generally believed to be the group's real talent. Their best original song was a three-minute rocker called 'I Don't Tan, I Burn'. On the flyers they handed out at their gigs they listed their influences as the Stones, Hendrix, Nirvana, Green Day, and the Beach Boys. They also did a cover of 'My Generation' by The Who. Their plan was to wait until their farewell gig – Brookfield's annual Battle of the Bands Night – and then trash their instruments as a finale to The Who cover. But the instruments were too expensive and the warning from the principal was too severe and in the end they didn't do it.

The boys did get into trouble fairly often, though. Struck by a new thought when they were drunk, they would pursue it without asking themselves whether or not it looked like a good idea. Some of their misadventures were essentially comic in spirit – or, at least, this was the tone they assumed in retrospect.

Like the time they hotboxed Barry Fox's second-hand Ford Fiesta and the guards knocked on the window.

Or the time they broke into a building site in Donnybrook and Dave Whelehan, drummer for the Paranoids, speared his foot on a rusty nail when he jumped off a wall without looking.

Or the time Richard sneaked into the school car park and stole a hubcap from the car of a visiting old boy who happened to be Ireland's star hooker for the coming season.

Or the time Barry squirted a carbon-dioxide fire extinguisher into a phone box on George's Street and walked out through the mist, staring at passers-by and shouting, 'WHAT YEAR IS THIS?'

Or the time Stephen and Richard burst into the Rape Crisis Centre on Dorset Street and shouted, 'WHO WANTS SOME?' at the waiting girls.

Talkin' 'bout my generation.

In April of sixth year Richard threw a graduation party at the house in Sandycove while Peter and Katherine were in Tenerife. In the pub beforehand Richard ended up inviting a bunch of people he'd never met before to the party. The house was wrecked. Tidying up the next day, Richard found a used condom next to his parents' bed. Half his mother's jewellery was missing. There were empty bottles everywhere and cigarette burns in the living-room carpet. Someone had upturned a bag of dog food in the utility room, which Peter Culhane, expecting a laugh every time, called the futility room. The freezer was unplugged and the wet linoleum was starting to curl at the edges. Richard ended up hiring professional cleaners and paid them with Peter's credit card.

Remember, these are bright, respectable young men. They did these things mostly so that they could talk about them afterwards.

This was what they talked about during nights of heavy drinking.

But these things happen to every rich kid in every city on earth. None of these stories offer an explanation for what happened to Conor. If you're looking for explanations, this is the wrong place to start.

This is an Irish story. Remember that. You have to be Irish to understand why it matters, why it makes a difference.

What makes Richard and Stephen and Barry different from any other group of rich young men, in any other country in the world?

For one thing, they were Irish Catholics: a puritanical breed. Only one newspaper picked up on this, as far as I can see, and they buried it in a feature article that came out during the trial. The Culhanes and the O'Briens and the Foxes were practising Catholics. They went to Mass every Sunday morning. They went to confession every three months. They had the parish priest over for coffee mornings. And in the central corridor of Brookfield College, there is a seven-foot-high statue of the Virgin Mary, her palms open, her eyes downcast in sorrow. I've seen it. It's right beside a trophy cabinet that holds ten consecutively dated Leinster Senior Cups, 1993–2003. Richard Culhane walked past the trophy cabinet and the sorrowful statue of the Virgin Mary every school day for six years.

When I start to wonder what the Culhanes do all day in the big white house on Inishfall, I think I know at least part of the answer. I think they pray.

Things they do look awful c-c-cold.

Peter Culhane consulted his credit card bill two weeks after he got back from Tenerife and told Richard he was grounded for a month. Richard was allowed out of the house once: to go to confession. He went to the chapel at Brookfield. Father Connelly absolved Richard of the mistake of the party and wished him good luck with the rugby.

Richard Culhane's graduation party at once became legendary. But Richard shrugged in irritation whenever it was mentioned. He didn't want to talk about it. It had become a private matter, something to be kept between Richard and his parents and God.

Conor Harris was at the graduation party too, of course. He was going out with Naomi Frears at the time. They were very much in love.

I hope I die before I get old.

7

They both played rugby but Richard was better. Conor was smaller and thinner than Richard, but he could run faster. Richard didn't need to be a runner. His size did most of the work for him. Conor played scrum half and Richard played fly half.

Richard wasn't short and squat like his father, and from a distance he didn't even look that powerful. But he had a tall, rangy athleticism that gave his every movement a kind of casual grace. And up close he was heavy and lithe.

He was comfortable with his own body, and it was this, I think, that fooled people into thinking his confidence was effortless.

'Christ,' Father Connelly said, the first time Richard walked out with the Brookfield Senior Cup team. 'That boy's built like a brick shithouse.'

Father Connelly was popular among the boys because of his foul mouth. But they took him seriously as a confessor, as a priest. He was one of the first people Richard, Stephen and Barry turned to on the morning they heard that Conor was dead.

I was there, too, the first time Richard walked out with the Senior Cup team. We all were. For that afternoon Richard Culhane was a hero to us. We wanted to be there beside him, every time he scored a point or made the conversion. There was a wistfulness about Richard, a glow of celebrity. He looked important. And he *was* important: important to us, and to the older men who loved the game and who wanted us to love it, too. If Richard could succeed, we thought but could not articulate, then we could all succeed, somehow. His talent made all of us feel more capable, more true.

Conor walked out with the Senior Cup team, too. I spotted him, head down, as he hustled from the dressing room. There was a frown of concentration on his face. But the photo that appeared in the next day's *Irish Times* was of Richard. The accompanying article said Richard's was 'the most promising debut in schools rugby in twenty-five years'.

Pat Kilroy, the principal of Brookfield, had this article framed and hung outside his office door.

And although it was Conor who scored the last try in the Senior Cup final that season, securing the match for Brookfield, it was Richard who made the conversion and was hoisted aloft and borne into the stands and sprayed with sparkling wine. It was Richard's face that we saw on the JumboTron screen, his hair soaked and a wide and slightly superior grin on his face.

I never heard anyone complain about this superior grin. Richard often smiled in just that way, usually when he thought no one was looking. People seemed to think that Richard Culhane deserved to feel superior. They seemed to think he *was* superior, in some forgivable way, in a way commensurate with his talents, his good looks, his popularity. His superiority made us love him all the more.

And Richard was good-looking. I never heard a girl say otherwise except in empty spite. The gel-spiked hair, the dense muscles in his chest, the lucid brown eyes. You saw him sitting in the café upstairs in the Quinn School of Business with one ankle propped on the opposite knee, wearing a blue-and-white striped Ben Sherman shirt with the collar turned up and a pair of grey O'Neills tracksuit bottoms, and you thought, *That guy could fuck any girl in this room.*

According to Barry Fox, who of the three Brookfield killers was the most inclined to gossip (before Conor's death, at least), Richard would sometimes be thinking this too. *I could fuck any girl in this room.*

It was true, objectively true. None of the girls in the Quinn School café, none of the girls with their bouffant hair and silver iPods, none of the girls in their pink American Eagle hoodies and sheepskin Ugg boots, would have thought of turning Richard down if, by some miracle, the beam of his attention became focussed on them. He was the most beautiful boy they had ever seen.

In his presence they became girly and flicked their hair. They listened to what he said. They laughed at his jokes.

Men felt strange around him, too. Beauty like Richard's leaves few people unmoved. In Brookfield he would be the object of the dreamy crushes of younger boys. Older men watched him closely when he was on the pitch.

It should have made him arrogant or obnoxious, but it didn't. He was proud of his beauty, but he kept the pride at a kind of ironic distance, as though his beauty was something for which he wasn't responsible. It gave him a sense of security, to know what kind of power he had and to decline the temptation to use it. Which is not to say that Richard didn't have a lot of sex. He did. But he was choosy about girls. They needed to have a certain look, a certain mode of speech, a certain quality of aloofness or lack of interest, before Richard would begin to be attracted. He was drawn to girls who treated clothes and music and movies with the same astute and genial condescension that he did, who acted as though they were humouring their less-well-developed friends by sharing their enthusiasms. What Richard really looked for in a girl was depth. What he looked for was the urge to *talk*.

'I like girls who *talk*, you know,' he told me once at a party.

I was recognized in those days as an authority on feelings, especially when it came to girls. I doubt Richard would have made this remark to anyone else.

Richard was very drunk. 'I like to know they take the whole relationship seriously, yeah?' he said. 'You have to *talk* about things. It's fucking crucial.' He leaned close to my face. 'My old pair,' he said in disgust. 'My old pair never talk. And that's the whole fucking problem. You know what I mean?'

Richard was always the centre of attention, wherever he went. But conversely, Richard seldom went anywhere that a good-looking schools rugby player *wouldn't* be the centre of attention. He stuck around college, or Eddie Rocket's in Donnybrook, or Brookfield, or the houses of his friends.

Richard's world was small. He liked it that way.

Here he is in the fifth-year class photo, with an angry red pimple on his chin. He's still the most handsome boy in his class of thirty. He's standing at the centre of the group, holding the Leinster Senior Cup trophy in front of him like a proud father with his firstborn.

People were always surprised that Richard did well at school, but he did. He got straight As in chemistry and biology. 'Richard was a pleasure to have in the class,' Mr Fogarty, the fat biology teacher, said to one of the papers. 'He was attentive, respectful and intelligent. I don't understand how this terrible thing could have happened. I still don't believe Richard could have had anything to do with it.'

Richard was a health freak, a fanatical anti-smoker. He worked hard in school. He made and drank a fruit smoothie with protein powder every morning and he always paid attention in class. Once some members of the sixth-year biology class, Barry Fox among them, stole a small quantity of ether from the school laboratory and tried to get high from the fumes in the wooded laneway that ran alongside the school. Richard was the one who found them. He smacked Barry Fox on the side of the head. 'What the fuck are you doing?' he shouted. 'Would you cop the fuck on to yourselves, for fuck's sake. This is no way to fucking behave.'

Barry said afterward, 'He actually scared me, like. He had this intensity in his eyes, like he was having a major fit or something. He really cared, you know? That we'd, like, betrayed the ethos of the school, or whatever. He was always loyal like that, you know. There was a line you didn't cross. It had something to do with respect. You respected the school, as far as Richard was concerned.'

We were all in love with Richard Culhane, I think. This is one of the things that made it so painful when we found out he'd helped to kill Conor.

8

The second thing that made the boys different from any other group of rich young men was that they were rich in a country that didn't know what to do about wealth. We weren't used to it, culturally speaking. And this causes problems. When you have a privileged class acting, as privileged classes will, as though their privilege were the most natural thing in the world, in a country where privilege still has the ring of the unnatural, of the undeserved, you have problems.

When the Irish economy (after seventy years of mismanaged independence) finally kicked into high gear, a whole new world sprang into being. This was the world of Brookfield and UCD, of Americanized slang and easy credit, of two-car families and cheap cocaine. This was a world in which, on any given evening, you could watch while a pyjamaed teenage girl with back-combed hair and furry boots jogged across the bleak forecourt of an all-night petrol station to buy a packet of safety razors to cut herself with. For generations our ruling class had been made up of landed Protestants, a genteel pseudo-aristocracy whose melancholy, long, withdrawing roar sounded well into the staid and steadfast 1950s. Their passing left a vacuum, a period of hesitancy and stagnation. Then, in the late 1990s, everything changed, everything thunderously convulsed. Suddenly – overnight, as it were – there was a new ruling class, a vast Catholic bourgeoisie, resident in a six-mile triangle of south County Dublin, who peopled the universities and the courts and the chambers of the government with capable and confident women and men.

Laura Haines and Richard Culhane and Conor Harris and all the others were scions of this class – a class that still exists, or seems to.

At least, people will tell you that it still exists. I wonder about this.

As late as the 1980s, certain sociologists were ready to classify Ireland as a Third World country – or, in the recent parlance, a Developing Nation. These days we're a Developed Nation. We're a First World country, now. With all the problems that entails.

As the twentieth century ended, we were doing something that no one else in Irish history had ever done. We were figuring out how to be rich.

And it hasn't ended yet. Ask anyone. Ask me, on a good day. Even as I write this account – even as I labour over this attempt to impose a form on the ineffable, on the defiantly formless – things still seem cosy, smooth, unendangered. Girls still wear their Ugg boots and their Prada perfume. Boys still play rugby for schools in leafy suburbs. Families still have two cars, utility rooms, wine cellars, Latvian maids to clean the kitchen.

We do know it will end, of course, our golden age, our belle epoque. At the edge of everything we do is the knowledge that this cocooned and happy little world, with all its desires and certainties, all its serene ambition, can't possibly last forever, that it will one day become something different, something that we'll find, waking one day in prosperous middle age, subtly unrecognizable. There are people, I know, who are waiting for the end, who are ready with their elegies and their funeral rites. But they're already too late. This world – rich south Dublin at the turn of the twenty-first century – is already over. It ended on the night of 31 August 2004. Even I see this only intermittently. But it's the truth.

A whole world died with Conor. We just haven't realized it yet.

Of course, the boys *themselves* weren't rich. They had rich parents, which isn't quite the same thing. The children of the rich, or so it seems, are free from anxieties about money. This seems to do something fundamental to their character.

Deep down, I think, the rich are uneasy about the deal they make with money. The deal is this: in exchange for good behaviour – in exchange for adhering without apparent effort to the codes and values of your class – you get to keep your money. Break the rules, and money is what you lose. It might be the last thing you lose, but it will always be the most important. This is why they go on, so many of them, amassing money. Why all their lives are spent amassing money.

We didn't invent money. Money invented us.

Peter Culhane made his deal with money early on. Right out of college he became an accountant for a large multinational firm of auditors and consultants. He was doing a more prestigious and remunerative version of this job when his son killed Conor Harris in August of 2004.

There were other aspects to Peter's deal. In 1976 he married Katherine Healy, his best friend's sister. Katherine wanted a registry-office wedding, but Peter said no. They talked about Katherine keeping her maiden name. The compromise they settled on was that Katherine's bank correspondence would be addressed to Katherine Healy-Culhane.

Peter was from what you call a lower-middle class background. His parents were primary school teachers who lived in Clonskeagh. This means that Peter Culhane wasn't born rich. His parents, Peter perceived as an adolescent, had never made any kind of deal with money. Unlike his son, Peter *did* have anxieties about what he earned. It seemed to do something fundamental to his character.

He studied Accounting at UCD. In those days you didn't do a Master's. From university – with the help of a lecturer who had studied at Brookfield – Peter was hired by the first of three multinationals to do, first, tax work, and later, auditing. The house in Sandycove had been in Katherine's family since the 1950s, and when Katherine's mother died (her father had died of leukemia before she was born), Peter and Katherine left their flat in Ballsbridge and moved to Sandycove. Katherine, six months pregnant with Richard, supervised the removal men while Peter was at work.

Katherine's family were richer than Peter's. They had made their money selling fish and dry goods. Katherine's brother Frank owned and operated a salmon-and-prawn processing plant on the north quays.

A month before Richard was born Peter drove up to Brookfield College in Blackrock and had a talk with the principal. Of course any old boy was welcome to visit. Of course Peter's son was guaranteed a place. With a flourish the principal (who, by the time of the events of my story, had long since retired) added the unborn Richard Culhane's name to the list of future entrants to the college. Peter came home and took his heavily pregnant wife into the bedroom and made love to her.

'I think everything's going to be alright,' he said when they had finished.

'Of course it will,' Katherine said, blinking.

The Culhanes gave money to charity and they donated their old clothes to the Vincent de Paul. They had tea in the Westbury every Christmas Eve. They observed, in a limited way, the Lenten fast. They went to the theatre (usually the Gate, seldom the Abbey) once a month. They drank in moderation. They paid a Polish maid to clean the house once a week.

By the time he built the swimming pool in the back garden Peter was earning one hundred and eighty thousand a year. Richard's school fees were eight thousand a year. Because he and Katherine had inherited their house, they never had to pay a mortgage.

Most marriages eventually look like a mistake. The Culhanes' was no exception. By the time Richard was sixteen Peter and Katherine were sleeping in separate bedrooms. It was generally supposed that Peter was having an affair but I never saw any evidence of this. Peter played a lot of golf in places like Druid's Glen and Mount Juliet and the K Club. His handicap was a nine, I believe. Two of the people he played golf with were Stephen O'Brien's father and Conor Harris's father. Before an important game – on Captain's Day, for example – Peter would take one of Katherine's prescription tranquillizers from their shelf in the bathroom cupboard. Before an important rugby match – if Brookfield were playing, or Ireland – Peter would swallow two capsules of St John's Wort, to calm himself down.

When Richard filled out his CAO form in February 2002 the second course he listed was Arts at UCD. The plan was that if Richard's Leaving Cert. results weren't up to standard, he could take

Economics and Maths as part of his Arts degree and go into a Master's in Business from there. The first course he listed on his CAO form was Business Accounting. This was run by the UCD Commerce faculty, which was, and still is, based in the Quinn School of Business on the Belfield campus of UCD, in an enormous white-concrete-and-glass building that looks like a grounded ocean liner.

Richard got 540 points in his Leaving Cert. It was one of the highest results in the year. At the Brookfield graduation ceremony that year he was given a medal for outstanding acheivement in Chemistry. In September 2002 Richard enrolled at the Quinn School of Business.

Both Barry Fox and Stephen O'Brien also went to UCD. Barry Fox was in the Quinn School, doing Management. Stephen O'Brien did Economics and Maths as part of his Arts degree. Stephen's minor subject was Psychology. 'All the fit birds do psychology,' he would observe as he sat in the Quinn School café. 'Look at her, man. I'd lash it into her.'

In the summer after he left school Richard got a job as an office boy at the company offices of a large firm of software manufacturers. Stephen O'Brien's father got him the interview, which was described as 'just a formality'.

'Sure keep us in mind when you've got the old degree in your arse pocket,' Maurice O'Brien said when Richard left to go to college.

Richard Culhane's future was immaculate. Of how many of us can that be so easily said?

9

The first time I saw Laura Haines was outside Simmonscourt Pavilion in Ballsbridge in the late May of 2003. The first thing I saw her do was take off the aviator shades she had been using as a hairband and pat down her hair to make sure it hadn't been disturbed. It was a perfect summer's day. Cars and trees and buildings looked spruce and clear in the afternoon light. Laura was carrying a green apple in her left hand and over her right shoulder was a pink Adidas rucksack. She was wearing three-quarter-length cut-off jeans in pale denim and a white string top that showed off her freckled shoulders. When she put the sunglasses on her face and looked up into the sun she looked impossibly aloof, impossibly beautiful, impossibly cool.

She also wore gold ballet pumps. She would be wearing these gold ballet pumps on the night Conor Harris died.

Simmonscourt Pavilion is a cavernous convention centre that belongs to the Royal Dublin Society. It's where the UCD exams are held at the end of every academic year. I had just come out of my final paper, and I was conscious of that strange sadness that always comes with the beginning of summer, with the apprehension that the next three months of perfect weather will contain nothing but work and wasted time.

The exam hall had been fusty with the generational airlessness of an old school classroom, but outside the sun shone and the air smelled of fresh-cut grass and sunstruck brick. Laura Haines, conspicuously alone, was standing by the main gate, waiting for a lift.

As I looked at her she began to eat the apple, her eyes unknowable behind the aviator shades.

Her final Radiography paper had gone badly. She would spend an hour that afternoon in the kitchen with her mother, working through her post-exam anxiety.

From a radio in the security guards' cabin by the main gate came a song, 'California' by Phantom Planet, that accompanied a popular TV series, a TV series to which Laura and her friends were at that time obsessively devoted.

Students filed past, jocular and brash, but I was watching Laura.

To some of us, Laura Haines seemed to embody everything that was good about our generation. She was confident and she had style. She was self-possessed. She was keenly aware of social distinctions. She was concerned about the environment and she was, I once heard someone say, 'very good with children'. She was also beautiful. Everyone at Brookfield wanted to fuck Laura Haines. Everyone at Merrion Academy wanted to fuck her, too. So did everyone at St Michael's and at Blackrock College and at Gonzaga. But you didn't dare to think that fucking Laura Haines would actually be possible. Fucking Laura Haines was something an entire generation of middle-class Dublin boys thought about entirely in the abstract.

Laura's popularity was of the kind that never seems likely to survive the end of school. In Laura's case it did. (Even fate, it seemed then, would make exceptions for Laura Haines.) She remained as aloof, beautiful and cool when she transferred to UCD, as she had been in fourth, fifth and sixth year at Ailesbury College. It seems likely that all the boys at UCD who knew Laura Haines wanted to fuck her. I don't know this for sure. Things become less clear when you get to college. Faced with all that blossoming individuality, you find it harder to successfully generalize. But Laura was the kind of girl who walked down the bustling hallway to a silent soundtrack of outraged groans – the suppressed sound that men make, the sound that roughly translates as, *That's not fair. Beauty that extreme just isn't fair.* So I'm sure everyone still wanted to fuck her, despite the multiplying variables.

I should make it clear that Laura Haines seldom fucked anybody.

She was neither frigid nor slutty. She dated boys and broke up with them and sometimes she slept with them and sometimes she didn't. Her sexual morality was as close to normal as you could get, in that time, at that place. Of course she had grown up in the same subtle, twilit world as all the other girls we knew, a world full of anxiety about sex (a worryingly invasive procedure, as far as fifteen-year-old Laura was concerned), a world nourished by Disney films and fairy tales, a world pointed towards the inevitably conjugal happy ending, and towards an odd practical sentimentality that mixed the robustly sensual with the dreamily fictitious. But Laura was the happy opposite of the frosty girls who walked with their arms folded, who demanded attention in ways that we could barely comprehend. Laura was forthright and slightly mysterious. Her beauty seemed to imply nothing hidden. Everything seemed to be on the surface.

(Of course, the group mind always simplifies things – and that's what I'm trying to conjure here, Laura as perceived by the group mind. But I'm simplifying things, too, as I go along. You should remember, as you read, that everything I say distils a plenitude of contradictions, that I am shaping and omitting, and that the truth around which I circle is, like all human truths, largely delusory to begin with.)

Since that moment outside Simmonscourt Pavilion, I've learned a great deal more about Laura Haines.

I've learned that she pronounced 'ground' and 'pound' as though they rhymed with 'grained' and 'pained'.

I've learned that she liked to dance to Justin Timberlake and OutKast and that she had a half-secret fondness for saccharine ballads like 'Total Eclipse of the Heart'. Her bedroom was still full of the CDs that had been popular when she was at school: Blur, Oasis, Pearl Jam. These groups were too boyish for her now.

I've learned that in school she had a mild eating disorder. By the time she arrived in UCD, she told Conor and later Richard, this had petered out to almost nothing.

I've learned that her eating disorder never really went away.

Laura's family lived in Ranelagh. She had gone to Ailesbury College, a private school for girls. Her mother had gone there, too.

I used to see the Ailesbury College students in their leaf-green uniforms as I walked into college in the early morning. They gathered in cliques at corners and bus stops to smoke. The fifth- and sixth-year girls went out on Friday nights, usually to clubs in Stillorgan or Temple Bar. On Saturday mornings they would get out of bed and, still wearing their pyjamas, convene in Coffee Society in Ranelagh for a gossip session about the events of the night before. Laura was always at the centre of these gossip sessions, even if, in her careful way, she made sure that none of the gossip was ever about her. People *told* Laura things. Girls confided in her. Of course Laura fell victim to a certain amount of the coded viciousness that feminine beauty reliably provokes in other girls. But I never heard anyone accuse her of cruelty or malice. Girls wanted her attention. They wanted her love, her kindness.

It still strikes me as odd that I had never met Laura Haines, had never even seen her in the flesh, as late as May of 2003. I'd heard people talk about her, of course. In the strangely limited way in which people can be famous in south Dublin, she was famous. I had seen photographs of her, what they call candid snapshots, taken on nights out with friends, photos passed around the web by people who knew people who knew people. This is how I recognized her when I saw her outside Simmonscourt Pavilion that afternoon.

In May of 2003, Laura Haines had just started going out with Conor Harris.

They met on Senior Cup final day. The final that year was Brookfield versus St Michael's. Brookfield took it with a miraculous conversion in the last minute. The biggest of the several celebrations that ensued took place in Kiely's in Donnybrook, late that afternoon.

Conor was walking from the coach that had brought the team from Lansdowne Road. He had ended up accompanying the team in the coach because of his celebrity status. Laura was with a gang of Brookfield supporters, Ailesbury College girls who were dating Brookfield boys. Laura was single at this time. She had been single for three months. Conor Harris and Laura Haines found themselves in the same crowd on the same street in Donnybrook as they walked towards Kiely's.

The street was full of people in the Brookfield colours, those strident reds and whites. Laura was wearing a red T-shirt and a short, white, ruffled skirt. She had a red plastic flower, a borrowed ornament, in her hair.

Laura and Conor began to talk on the street. They didn't know each other's names. This is perhaps the most amazing thing, that of all the people on that crowded street, it should have been Laura and Conor who found one another. They had dozens of mutual friends. People have said, in vibrant tones, that they were destined to be together.

By the end of the night they had kissed.

By the end of the week they were a couple.

This was in late April, 2003.

I have no idea what they talked about as they walked along that street in Donnybrook. I do know that Conor, in an impulsive moment, reached up and took the red plastic flower from Laura's hair and put it in his own. He woke up the next morning, still wearing all his clothes, with the red plastic flower clutched in his left hand. In fact, he kept it, hiding it in his wardrobe and telling only one other person about the flower and what it meant to him.

Laura was the girl on Richard Culhane's arm on the last night of summer, 2004.

She was wearing her gold ballet pumps and a black hoodie spangled with silver stars. She wore the hoodie because she was cold and she had worn only a short blue summer dress to the club that night.

(Laura had worn this dress only once before, to her Ailesbury College Pre-Debs, and anyone who had seen her wearing it tended to tell anyone who hadn't that they had missed out, big time.)

So Laura was wearing the black star-spangled hoodie, and beneath it you could see the end of her dress and her bare legs and the gold ballet pumps.

And Conor Harris found Richard Culhane in the crowd.

When the punches started and Conor fell to the ground and six to ten people surrounded him and started kicking, Laura backed away until she fell against a parked car. Later she said she thought she was about ten feet away from the fight.

At the first trial she testified that she thought she'd been shouting throughout the attack, shouting at the boys to stop, shouting at Richard to come away, shouting at Barry and Stephen to leave Conor alone.

She said she wasn't able to identify any of the other boys who were involved in the kicking.

She said she saw blood spattering across the concrete path.

She said she saw Conor fall. His head struck the ground with a terrible wet smack.

She shouted to the boys to stop.

They seemed to be a long way away.

When they had stopped – and all of this, remember, happened in less than a minute, took maybe thirty seconds, fifty at the most – and Richard staggered back with a glassy look in his eyes and Barry Fox, after a pause of unspecified duration, knelt and touched Conor's head to see if he was breathing, Laura said she remembered saying, 'This can't be happening.' She said she repeated it and realized she was crying.

This can't be happening. This can't be happening.

Blood on the concrete and on Conor's clothes. Blood on Richard's trainers and on the Ben Sherman shirt he wore. Everyone out of breath and exhilarated.

A lot of blood on Conor's face.

It may have been at this point that Stephen O'Brien said, 'We fucking showed that little cunt.'

Various people claimed to have heard Stephen O'Brien say various things. This is the version that seems to have been agreed upon. This is the version produced by consensus.

We fucking showed that little cunt.

This can't be happening.

Laura said that the next morning she looked at the star-spangled hoodie and found that it was covered in blood. The DPP has theorized that Laura was standing much closer to the fight than she remembered. They have also theorized that the blood on the hoodie came from Richard Culhane's fist, which was damaged during the fight. DNA tests might have shown who the blood belonged to, but

Laura washed the hoodie as soon as she woke up, and no traces of the blood remained. She washed it even before Richard Culhane arrived at her house to tell her that Conor was dead.

Like everybody else, I think the blood was Conor's. But I don't know this for sure.

At the trial Laura was asked if she had seen Richard Culhane deliver the third and final kick (*bang*) to Conor's head. She said she couldn't remember. But I think she saw it. I think she saw that kick. I think she was one of the people who were privately convinced – convinced beneath the public need, the clamour, for decorum – that Richard's kick had been the fatal one.

Of course I knew about none of this that afternoon outside Simmonscourt Pavilion when I stood, fiddling with a cigarette and covertly admiring Laura Haines as she stood in cool repose, finishing her apple and putting the core into a pocket of her Adidas rucksack.

She was waiting for Richard Culhane. He had offered her a lift home from her last exam. Conor was busy that day. What was he doing? Nobody remembers; I have no way of finding out. My story is full of gaps. All I have are theories.

I saw Richard's car swing into the Pavilion gateway. He had the windows down and his muscular right arm rested on the hot metal of the doorframe. He was smoking a cigarette. This last detail was so odd, so out of character, that I wondered for a minute if it was really him, if perhaps he had loaned his car to some other Brookfield boy for the afternoon. But no: it was Richard. He too wore aviator shades, and he smiled at Laura as the car slowed and stopped, and as she walked around the bonnet to get to the passenger door Richard dropped the cigarette, half-smoked, on to the ground beneath his window.

Laura got into the car and for a moment they sat there, affectless as godlings, inscrutable behind their sightless silver shades.

I wanted to be them. I wanted to be both of them, Laura as much as Richard. They were so completely of their time and place, so sure of themselves and so beautiful, that I could only envy them. I envied them their immediate future: the exam post-mortem in the comfy kitchen, the drinks in Harry's later on that night. And I envied them their lives, those perfect, glancing, stylish lives that only they seemed fit to lead.

In retrospect, this scene leaves me troubled. There are too many unanswered questions.

Why was Laura with Richard, when she had just started to go out with Conor Harris?

Why was Richard smoking a cigarette, when he had always hated the very idea of smoking?

Why did they sit there in silence in the car, as the students walked past, not looking at each other, not speaking?

I have no answers.

This can't be happening.

This can't be happening.

Bang. Bang. Bang.

10

During Conor's first year at Brookfield Brendan Harris drove his son to school every morning on his way to work. The family had two cars: a brand-new Renault Megane hatchback that belonged to Eileen and a ten-year-old Audi 800 that belonged to Brendan. For the school run, Conor went with Brendan in the Audi.

After a couple of weeks Conor started asking to be dropped at the corner of Mount Merrion Avenue, a couple of hundred yards from the school gates. He said he wanted to walk the rest of the way. Brendan said, 'That's ridiculous, Conor. I'm driving in that direction anyway.'

'But *Dad*,' Conor said.

This was a morning in late September 1997 and it was raining heavily. The windscreen wipers went back and forth.

'If I were you I'd *want* to be dropped right to the school gates,' Brendan said. 'Especially on a morning like this.'

'But I don't want people to *see*.'

'You don't want people to see *what*?'

They were passing St Vincent's Hospital. Puddles had formed by the kerbs.

Conor looked out of the window and mumbled something.

'What?' Brendan said.

'The *car*,' Conor said. 'I don't want people to see the *car*.'

'What's wrong with the car?' Brendan said, piqued.

'It's *old*,' Conor said.

'*Old?*'

'It's ten years old. All the other guys' dads have, like, '97-reg. cars. Yours is way the oldest car in the car park.'

Brendan pulled the car over. The windscreen wipers kept going back and forth.

'Right so,' Brendan said.

'Right so what?'

'If you're actually ashamed to be seen in my car then you might as well get out and walk from here.'

Conor looked around. Rain came off the kerbside puddles in foot-high splashes. It would take him fifteen minutes to walk to Brookfield.

He looked at Brendan to see if he was joking.

Brendan stared straight ahead between the windscreen wipers.

After a few minutes Brendan pulled back out into the traffic. Neither he nor Conor said anything until they reached the gates of the school.

'Bye, Dad,' Conor said.

'I'll pick you up at four,' Brendan said.

Conor was thirteen years old.

Two years later Brendan Harris sold the Audi and bought a 1999-reg. BMW. I think Conor was very pleased about this, but I don't remember him ever mentioning it out loud.

11

Laura Haines wasn't Conor's first girlfriend, not by any means. You don't play rugby for Brookfield College and not have lots of girls.

Kissing a girl on a night out was called scoring. Conor scored with some regularity, but, like almost all the other boys on the Senior Cup team, he rarely slept with anyone. Dublin private-school girls are tetchy about their virginity. 'A few blow jobs in the bushes,' was how Conor once summed up the sexual experiences he had had before college.

Of course, like Richard Culhane and Laura Haines, he regularly went to the Wesley Disco in Donnybrook. The Wesley Disco is mainly frequented by people in first, second and third year of secondary school. After the Junior Cert. it becomes uncool to go to the Wes. Most of Conor's blow jobs in the bushes probably happened after a night at the Wes.

'Were you at the Wes on Friday night?' would go the typical conversation among Brookfield third years on a Monday or Tuesday morning.

'Yeah, I was there for a while.'

'You score?'

'I got a handjob from this chick.'

'Oh yeah? She hot?'

'She was a fuckin' dog, man.'

Laughter, high fives.

Girls don't wear their underwear to the Wesley Disco. They take their thongs off in the bathroom at the beginning of the night. When they see a guy they like, they walk up to him and hand him the thong.

Scoring random girls had a certain cachet but Brookfield boys are respectful of the institution of the girlfriend. Conor was more sceptical than most about the idea of committing to a girl.

Nonetheless, Conor had several girlfriends. The one that made the deepest impression, before Laura came along and obliterated everyone else, was a girl from Belfast called Naomi Frears. Naomi was the girl Conor took to his Debs.

The Debs is a social ritual of immense importance in the Dublin private-school system. Schools nominate committees of students every year to set them up. By tradition, the Brookfield Debs is held in the Killiney Court Hotel, which is perched on a hill above the DART line and overlooks Killiney Bay.

Naomi Frears was a St Anne's College, Foxrock, girl. (Joke: What does a St Anne's girl do first thing in the morning? Goes home.) Conor met her in Russell's in Ranelagh one night after a Senior Cup game. He picked her up at her house before the Debs. He brought flowers and chocolates for Naomi's mother. That was the way it was done.

Before they left for the Killiney Court Conor and Naomi posed for the traditional Debs photograph in the living room of the Frears' house in Goatstown. Here is the photo in its gilded frame: Conor looks awkward and pimply in his rented tux, Naomi is small and frail in a short black dress of some velvety material. They both smile with unaffected pride.

This was the most widely disseminated photograph of Conor during the months of the controversy and the trial.

In the picture he looks like a big man. But he wasn't as tall as Richard Culhane and he wasn't as strong as Stephen O'Brien.

I look at this picture often, because it seems to capture a moment of tranquillity, of justified complacency. It shows two young people who have no idea what is going to happen to them and no conviction that anything will ever change. I look at this picture often because I know what happened later that night.

Everyone gets very drunk at a Debs. Although the girls have

spent weeks getting ready and the boys have spent two hundred quid on a tux and some flowers, the purpose of the evening is to get as drunk as you can as quickly as you can.

Conor was a heavy drinker. Even by the standards of his class and generation, Conor was a heavy drinker. It seldom did him any harm. But at the Brookfield Debs, he overdid it. I can tell you exactly what he drank that night, because he told me all about it. Before he even left the house he and Fergal Morrison, his closest friend at Brookfield, had shared a half-bottle of Smirnoff vodka. At the Debs itself Conor and Fergal matched each other drink for drink: Two glasses of wine at dinner, six pints of Guinness, a White Russian, three gin and tonics, a shot of sambuca, two shots of Jägermeister, two bottles of Miller. By this stage Conor's eyelids were swollen and he was shouting a lot. Somehow he got into conversation with Sarah O'Dwyer. Sarah O'Dwyer was Fergal Morrison's date for the Debs. Somehow Conor ended up scoring Sarah. Fergal staggered back from the bathroom and saw them kissing in a corner by an empty table.

'WHAT THE FUCK ARE YOU DOING, MAN?' Fergal screamed, more in amusement than in anger. He was very drunk.

Conor refused to apologize.

Fergal waved Naomi over.

When Naomi realized what had happened, she started to cry.

Conor stared at Fergal and shouted, 'WHAT THE FUCK DID YOU DO THAT FOR, YOU PRICK!' He put his palms on Fergal's chest and shoved.

Fergal fell backwards.

Conor made to jump on top of him but some Brookfield boys grabbed him by the arms and told him to calm the fuck down.

'I'll fucking kick your face in,' Conor shouted at Fergal. 'And your fucking bird's, too. She is one fucking ugly bitch, man. You can fucking have her.'

Fergal agreed to take Sarah home. Naomi said she would call a taxi. Conor stopped her by the door. He apologized for a long time.

'I'll throw myself on the tracks,' Conor screamed at her. 'Is that what you fucking want?'

'The DART's not running, man,' someone said.

'I'll go down to the tracks and fucking lie there. Do you want me to do that? I'll do that for you, Naomi. I fucking love you, alright?'

Conor had started to cry.

Someone said, 'I'm telling you, man, the train's not running for like another four hours. You'll be lying there a long time.'

Naomi said she would forgive Conor if he let her go home.

After Naomi had left, Conor went to the bathroom to throw up. Then he sat in a cubicle and cried for half an hour.

There was an incident with the bouncers when Conor tried to leave. Conor tried to start a fight in the foyer. The bouncers were very tolerant. They put him in a taxi and told him to fuck off home.

In the words of certain people – spoken after the fact, after Conor was dead – 'Conor Harris was no angel.' During the trial, these words were uttered in various places: in Gleeson's in Booterstown, where Peter Culhane and Maurice O'Brien often went to drink; at dinner parties and in offices and in the waiting rooms of costly clinics; even in newspaper offices (though never in print). Nobody said it on the record. It was very much the unofficial view. And, like all unofficial views, it expressed a valid if partial truth.

This is something that certain people haven't wanted to acknowledge about Conor Harris.

Sometimes, he could be a real cunt.

12

When I talk about the boys' parents, I realize I'm talking about a certain kind of person. The Culhanes and the O'Briens and the Foxes were people who knew people. Or they knew people who knew people. They didn't quail before the world's complexity. They knew how to cope. They knew people at *The Irish Times* and the *Evening Herald.* They knew people at Deloitte & Touche and they knew people at Microsoft. They knew people at Intel and Lucent Technologies and Independent News and Media. They knew people at Trinity and UCD. They knew barristers and accountants and TDs. They knew people who played golf with the Minister for Justice or the Minister for Arts, Culture and the Gaeltacht. They knew people at RTÉ. They knew neurosurgeons at Vincent's and paediatricians at Mater Dei. They knew their local bishop and they had drinks with their local GP. They drank in the Horseshoe Bar of the Shelbourne Hotel or in Doheny & Nesbitt's, and they ate at Chapter One or Roly's Bistro. They went antiquing in Dalkey or they went to the Farmers' Market in Leopardstown. They shopped at Brown Thomas and Habitat and Laura Ashley. All of these superficial things – all of these things about where to shop and where to eat and where to drink – were an aspect of knowing people, of knowing how the world worked, or of thinking you knew how it worked.

Eileen and Brendan Harris were the exceptions to all of this. Eileen Harris, née Houlihan, was born and grew up in County Carlow, on a farm owned and operated by her parents. Brendan Harris grew up in

Kilkenny town. They were never a part of the Dublin private-school system. They met each other the morning after a friend's party. Eileen was eighteen and Brendan was twenty-two. This was in August of 1975. How they made their money was through the restaurant they opened in Dublin in June of 1982. Conor was born two years later, on 20 January 1984. Eileen and Brendan ran the restaurant hands-on for seven years before they paid a manager to take over and began to develop the franchise around Dublin. The restaurants that resulted weren't particularly upscale but they weren't particularly downscale, either. The Harrises bought a six-bedroom house in Donnybrook and supervised the running of the four restaurants they owned.

The initial investment for the first restaurant had come from Eileen's parents. So in a sense the Harrises had money from the start. But they didn't have money the way Peter Culhane and his wife had money. The Harrises were reluctant to spend their money, and they stayed reluctant for twenty years. They would never build a swimming pool in the back garden, for instance. They were afraid to turn their money into tangible goods. They preferred to keep it liquid.

But they did send their son to Brookfield.

They could easily afford the fees of eight thousand a year, of course. They could easily have afforded the slightly larger amount it would have cost to send Conor to board at Clongowes Wood in County Kildare, where Brendan's father had wanted to send him. But Brendan Harris had always been attracted to what he saw as the austerity and refinement of the Dublin rugby schools. He saw Brookfield as Conor's way into the establishment, into the kind of life where comfort and authority are taken for granted, where it is accepted that one will know neurologists at Vincent's, paediatricians at Mater Dei.

It was also about sport. Brendan wanted Conor to make the Senior Cup team. After a while, Conor wanted it, too.

Of course, it made a difference that Conor's father hadn't gone to Brookfield. It made a difference to how he was seen by the other boys. There was always something of the outsider about Conor Harris, some air of dissatisfaction. People at Brookfield nursed the lingering suspicion that because Conor's parents weren't from Dublin, because they had made their money in the service industry,

Conor simply wasn't comfortable being rich, that he wasn't comfortable at Brookfield. You could occasionally see that Conor was aware of this. On the rugby pitch, training in the leaden afternoons, he would charge a bit too heavily, run for slightly too long, exhaust himself and grow frustrated at his own exhaustion, at his own apparent unsuitability for where he was and what he was doing.

But this happened rarely, and you could only see it if you were looking for it.

You could see it in Brendan and Eileen Harris, too.

Brendan played golf at Mount Juliet and Druid's Glen and the K Club, but he never, I think, felt that he particularly belonged at these places. It was an effort of will that kept him there – the same force of will that kept Peter Culhane and Maurice O'Brien and John Fox from quailing before the world's complexity, but narrower somehow, more constrained.

Brendan Harris liked to cook. There was something private, even hobbyist, about Brendan when he was cooking. He liked to make duck à l'orange with shallots and parsnips. 'I may never get a Michelin star,' he would say, 'but as long as I enjoy myself, that's all that matters.' He always sounded unconvincing when he said this, like a man verbally auditioning a philosophy he had already rejected; or like a man trying to deny a larger insecurity.

The most interesting story I've heard about Eileen Harris was about the time Brendan took her to his parents' twenty-fifth wedding anniversary party in a hotel in Kilkenny town. Eileen was working in a florist's in Carlow. She was so intimidated by the prospect of presenting Mary Harris, her new boyfriend's mother, with a bronze picture frame, that she waited until Mary was in the bathroom and passed the present, along with its card, under the gap beneath the toilet-cubicle door.

The Harrises loved their son. I can't make that clear enough. They loved Conor more than I can easily express. But they were parents. What else do parents do?

They loved their son. That's why they were so angry when he died and no one seemed willing to shoulder the blame.

13

Once – just once – I had coffee with Laura Haines and two of her friends from Ailesbury College. The friends were called Elaina Ross and Rebecca Dowling. We sat outside Café Moda in Rathmines one morning in February, 2004. I felt the privileged awkwardness of being the only boy at a table of rich young women.

Elaina was blonde and thin. She studied Business at Trinity. Rebecca studied Psychology at UCD. Rebecca was one of those comparatively fat, plain girls who act as crutches for their pretty, blonde best friend.

I was struck by how little Laura contributed to the conversation. But she did announce that she had met a new boy. With characteristic modesty she refrained from mentioning that it was Richard Culhane.

Even at the time I found this odd. I was aware that Laura already knew Richard Culhane, because I had seen him pick her up from outside Simmonscourt Pavilion the previous summer.

I didn't know why she would lie about having just met him.

Of all the people in this story, Laura's motivations are the most opaque. Her role in the events that led to Conor's death barely made the papers. I found this odd, too, because she had been the love of Conor's life for the guts of a year. But the papers had their own ideas about Conor's death. It was an indictment of our binge-drinking culture. It was prosperity gone mad. It was a family tragedy. It was all of the above.

I don't think Laura is to blame for Conor's death. But I do think she had more to do with it than the certain sections of the media have chosen to acknowledge.

Laura's role is a strange one. I'm still not clear about it myself.

But I was there when Laura first mentioned that she had found a new boyfriend. She mentioned it obliquely but I could tell, by her silence and her smile, that something significant was going on.

The girls, that day, were remembering their Debs.

'Could you *believe* how many Mounties were there?' Elaina said, spooning foam from the surface of her cappuccino and leaving it in her saucer ('All the calories are in the foam,' she had told me once, as though in confidence). 'Oh my God. It wasn't even *their* Debs. It was like a *combined* Debs. The schools should have them together. Like when I was in sixth year they drove my whole class down to Clongowes in a coach so we could score Clongowes boys, or they could score us, I wasn't sure which. They set up a disco or whatever to make it all look above board, but everybody knew the real reason.' She took a sip and crossed her legs. She wore bootcut Levis and calf-length leather boots with three-inch heels. 'But seriously. They shouldn't let Mount Anville people gatecrash the Ailesbury College Debs. It's ridiculous. They should have got, like, security, or something.'

'Totally,' Rebecca said.

'The Mounties did bring some gorgeous guys,' Elaina said. 'I mean *gorgeous*. But they behaved *so badly*. I just couldn't believe it. Like this one guy threw up all down the front of Natasha O'Connor's Debs dress. I mean, fine if it's an ordinary dress for a night out or whatever. But you don't vomit all over someone's Debs dress. It's just *not* on.'

'Didn't you, like, score that guy?' Laura asked.

'That was *before*,' Elaina said crossly.

Laura and Elaina had been on the cake committee for their Debs at Ailesbury College. Because of the number of Brookfield boys who had been invited to attend (I had heard a rumour, possibly satirical in origin, that in a certain sixth-year class at Ailesbury College a year or two ago, every single girl had been going out with a Brookfield boy), there had been some debate about the cake's design. Every year the cake was decorated with the Ailesbury College colours: green and white. This year, several girls – including Laura – on the cake committee had suggested adding a section in Brookfield red and white. The debate had become so heated that eventually the school authorities had been forced to step in and assert that the Ailesbury College cake should bear the Ailesbury College colours and nothing else. Bitterness about this affair still lingered, two years later, and when Ailesbury College girls from that year got together, sooner or later they would start to talk about the cake.

Elaina consulted her mobile phone. 'Didn't you score Richard that night?' she said.

'At the Debs? Yeah, right,' Laura said. 'He was going out with, like, Claire Lawrence.'

'Yeah, but he took you to your Debs.'

'I just met someone, actually,' Laura said.

'Where did he go to school?' Rebecca asked.

'That's for me to know,' Laura said.

'That means we know him,' Elaina said. 'We've probably, like, scored him or something.'

Elaina and Rebecca laughed together, though I sensed in Rebecca's effortful chuckle some pain at the fact that, whoever Laura's new boyfriend was, Rebecca would almost certainly not have scored him.

'He says I have soulful eyes,' Laura said, nettled.

'Doesn't sound like anyone I've ever hooked up with,' Elaina said.

'Me either,' I said, and achieved my aim of getting a laugh and distracting Laura from Elaina's curiosity.

Laura punched me on the arm. 'Bet you'd like them to say that, though, wouldn't you?' she said. 'You're just a big romantic.'

Elaina ordered a Caesar salad which she insisted she would share with Rebecca. Laura asked for another coffee. They chattered amiably. They flirted with the waiter.

Elaina chewed a leaf of lettuce. 'Did you see they've got Uggs in the Dundrum Town Centre for like, a hundred and fifty quid? I think that's amazing.'

Rebecca said, 'I thought you didn't like Uggs.'

'Well, you know, I've come around.'

I don't know whether Richard ever actually told Laura that she had soulful eyes. Possibly this was something he had said to her back at the beginning of Laura's first year at UCD, when after a summer apart they ran into each other one night in the Forum Bar after the Literary and Historical Society debate on prostitution. If so, it wasn't up to the standards of Richard's usual come-ons.

Why didn't Laura tell the girls she had finally started going out with Richard Culhane?

Why did she tell them something about him that was months or even years out of date?

I ended up driving Laura into college from Rathmines. I thought about asking her if the boy she had met was Richard. But I knew it was. I knew because Conor had already seen them together, on the dance floor at the Bondi Beach Club in Stillorgan, and he had told me all about it.

14

In his six years at Brookfield, Richard got in trouble only once. Because of Richard's 'outstanding reputation as a player and a student', Pat Kilroy suspended him for only a single day, instead of for the full week mandated by the school's code of conduct. He also invited Peter Culhane to come into his office for a chat.

What had happened was this. During a Senior Cup qualifier, in the last minute of the first half, Richard had the ball and was barrelling towards the post, eight or nine yards from the line. The game was Brookfield against a Tallaght CBC. Three yards out, Richard was tackled by a hooker from the Tallaght side. It was a heavy tackle, above the waist. Richard lay on the pitch for sixty seconds after the whistle blew, convinced his jaw was broken.

In the locker room he said nothing. He didn't respond to the outraged condolences of Barry Fox and Fergal Morrison. He sat there and drank his water and when the second half began he waited until the Tallaght hooker had the ball and tackled him as hard as he could, aiming for the small of the back. It was a head-first lunge, a savage sprawl of lowered shoulders and flailing limbs. The CBC player went down. Richard braced himself against the ground and delivered three thick punches (*bang bang bang*) to the other boy's neck and shoulders before the ref and some Brookfield boys pulled him free. The ball was Brookfield's and Conor Harris kicked it clear for the line-out.

The CBC boy had a black eye and some damage (it was later confirmed) to the cartilage in his left shoulder. Richard was sent off. He didn't stay for the rest of the match. He didn't even take a shower. He grabbed his bag from the locker room and drove home to Sandycove.

'Richard came in too hard on the tackle,' was the consensus view of this incident.

'*Way* too hard,' Fergal Morrison later said. 'He wasn't *tackling* that guy. He was trying to fucking *bury* him.'

Pat Kilroy was forced to reprimand Richard for bringing the good standing of the school into disrepute.

'What were you *thinking*, Richard?' he asked.

This was the following day. Richard sat in Kilroy's office in his school uniform with its red-and-white tie.

'I just lost it,' Richard said. Throughout the interview with Pat Kilroy his face was red and his throat felt ticklish and constricted. He found that enjoying Pat Kilroy's respect was a crucial part of his own self-belief.

'You just lost it,' Pat Kilroy said. He exhaled through his nose. 'We've never had trouble like this from you before, Richard.'

Richard's attack on the CBC player had been recorded on some-body's camera-phone, and he had watched the footage. It seemed to him that someone else had taken control of his body during those few violent seconds. But he also remembered that he had taken pleasure in this sensation. He had wanted to hurt his own body, too. He had wanted to keep going until he himself was bleeding and the other boy was dead.

There was something else he had enjoyed. He had enjoyed nursing a grudge about his injured jaw. He had enjoyed sitting tensely in the locker room, ignoring his friends, feeling an iron spring of righteous anger tighten itself in his chest.

He knew the iron spring had always been there.

'I'm sorry, sir,' he said to Pat Kilroy.

'I know you are, Richard, I know you are.'

'But he did tackle me first.' Richard thought he sounded grown-up, reasonable.

'It was a dirty tackle, I know that.'

'He tackled me first and he nearly broke my jaw.'

Pat Kilroy went to the window of his office and looked out at the single copper beech tree on the college lawn.

'I'm talking about *ethos*, here, Richard,' he said. 'I'm talking about being a man. I'm talking about not stooping to the level of our baser cousins. We rise above, Richard. That's what makes us worthwhile human beings.'

This speech meant a lot to Richard Culhane. He wanted above all to be a worthwhile human being.

Later that week Peter Culhane visited Pat Kilroy.

'There was a provocation,' Pat Kilroy said. 'I can understand why Richard responded the way he did. But the fact is, he shouldn't have done it. He should have been able to control himself. I mean, we're lucky that boy wasn't more seriously injured.'

Peter held his head at a pious angle. 'It's true, Pat. But, you know, Richard's a proud young man. He doesn't like taking a knock. He feels he has to stand up for himself.'

'Well he *does*,' Pat Kilroy said. 'He does have to stand up for himself. But he has to choose his battles.'

'I'll have a word with him,' Peter said.

'You do that,' said Pat Kilroy.

Then the two men went into the hallway to look at a photograph of the Senior Cup team that Peter Culhane had played with, twenty-three years ago to the season.

I should explain that boys get knocked or kicked unconscious during schools rugby matches all the time. It isn't common, exactly, but it happens. It happens most frequently during matches in which Brookfield College are playing.

Brookfield is the only schools team whose supporters habitually boo the opposition when they run out on to the pitch. This is regarded by teams from other schools as 'arrogant' and 'not fair play'.

Richard's attack on the CBC boy contributed to his status as a legend among schools players. It also contributed to the mystique he conjured in the eyes of women. For a while he posted the camera-phone footage of the fight on his Bebo page. He took it down eventually because he was afraid it made him look like a cunt.

This confuses me. Although Richard was deeply affected by Pat

Kilroy's exhortations, and was therefore deeply ashamed of his actions on the pitch that day, he still posted the footage on the web for his friends to see.

Of course, it is possible to be both proud and ashamed of your behaviour.

We fucking showed that little cunt.

For a short while a rumour circulated to the effect that the CBC boy got what he deserved because, in the first minute of the second half, he had made a joke about fucking Richard's mother. Richard always insisted that this wasn't the case. He insisted that he had merely been retaliating for the dirty tackle in the first half. And people accepted what he said.

My point is this: everyone forgave Richard for his loss of temper on the pitch. Some of us disapproved of it. Some of us thought it was cool. But everyone forgave it. There was never any question about that.

15

This fall, Conor's fall. People have talked about this over and over again. Could the fall alone have killed him? Could the damage done when his head struck the pavement have been the moment of irreversible damage, the moment when Richard and Stephen and Barry stopped being people and started being killers, or victims of a violent drink-culture, or spoilt thugs with no idea of the consequences of their actions? Were the kicks irrelevant? Was Conor already dead?

This is just one more thing I can't answer. If anything, these questions leave us with still more questions. If Conor fell, who was responsible? Who knocked him down? Was he floored by a massive punch from Stephen O'Brien or Barry Fox? Did he hug himself to shelter from the blows and lose his balance? Did he throw himself at the ground to keep himself from the fists of his attackers?

The state pathologist's report isn't helpful here. According to the report, no evidence could be found that would help to reconstruct the exact course of the fight. All we're left with is a series of conflicting eyewitness accounts.

Most fights, especially if the people involved are drunk, tend to be over in a few seconds. According to the DPP, the best evidence they could put together indicated that six to ten people punched and kicked Conor Harris for almost a minute.

Six to ten.

There are maybe seven people still out there who were involved in the fight that killed Conor. The guards could only manage to identify three of the assailants.

Richard was identified by a taxi driver.

Stephen and Barry were identified by several different people who claimed that they saw Stephen and Barry throw most of the punches.

Most of the witnesses who testified at the trial couldn't remember seeing Laura Haines stumble against a parked car as she backed away from the fight. But one man did see it happen. This is because the car she stumbled against was an idling taxi, and the driver was sitting at the wheel.

Laura obscured his view of the fight, the driver told the guards, but he did see Richard Culhane walk away as the fracas ended. He saw Richard walk over to the cab and put his arm out to Laura Haines. Laura seemed upset, but the driver couldn't hear what she was saying because the window on that side of the car was rolled up.

The taxi driver got out of the car and leaned on the roof.

'Here,' he said to Richard, and nodded over at Conor. 'Is that fella alright?'

At this point, most people are agreed, Stephen O'Brien shouted, 'We fucking showed that little cunt.'

Richard said to the taxi driver, 'Can you take us home?'

'I think you should stay and look after your friend.' The driver gestured at Laura. 'Could you get off the car, please, love?' he said.

The taxi driver – his name was Mick Conroy – left Blackrock and drove to pick up a fare in Booterstown and then into the city centre. He then drove back to Blackrock because, he said, 'I was concerned about the young fella. He'd just been lyin' there, like.'

When he got back – this was forty-five minutes later – Conor was still lying on the concrete of the path. At this point he was still breathing. Fergal Morrison and Dave Whelehan were sitting beside him. Debbie Guilfoyle, Dave's girlfriend, stood nearby with two friends. They were all dialing numbers on their mobile phones.

The taxi driver asked the girls what they were doing. They were all trying to raise taxis to take Conor home, they said.

'It's not home he needs,' the taxi driver said.

The taxi driver called an ambulance.
It arrived forty minutes later.

16

Bang.

    Bang.

    Bang.

When Conor had fallen and the kicking had stopped, Barry Fox was the one who knelt and touched Conor's head to see if he was okay.

Later, at the trial, he testified that Conor was still breathing as far as he could tell.

It is probable that brain damage had already occurred by the time Barry watched Conor's chest to see if he was still breathing. The report of the state pathologist would indicate that inhalation of blood was a substantial contributing factor in Conor's subsequent death. In the report the actual cause of death is listed as massive internal haemorrhaging in the area of the frontal lobe. But when Barry Fox knelt to check on him, Conor was still breathing. He was still alive.

This would have been about twenty minutes after three on Sunday morning.

'Christ,' Barry said. 'I think we should call an ambulance. Guys, I fucking think we should call an ambulance.'

He was still kneeling over Conor's body and looking up into the crowd. He says he doesn't remember who he was talking to when he said, 'I think we should call an ambulance.' It's logical to assume he was talking to Richard Culhane and Stephen O'Brien, and possibly even to Laura Haines, who was still leaning against Mick Conroy's idling car, dressed in her bloodstained black hoodie. But in a sense it doesn't matter who Barry was talking to at this point, because nobody called an ambulance until it was almost five o'clock in the morning, and by then it was much too late.

While Barry was kneeling to check if Conor was still alive, Stephen O'Brien was shouting and thumping the tops of cars parked along the Blackrock main street.

There was, of course, no garda presence in Blackrock that night. Questions were asked in the papers and at the trial about this. No explanations were forthcoming.

While Barry was kneeling to check if Conor was still alive, Richard Culhane went to talk to Laura Haines. He put his arm on her shoulder. She shrugged him away. She was crying.

'Oh, you think you're such a big man,' she said. Her face was wet and shiny in the streetlights. 'You think you're such a big fucking man, Richard.'

This can't be happening. This can't be happening.

Richard looked at Stephen O'Brien, who was standing in the middle of the street, crowing and jumping up and down. He looked at Barry Fox, kneeling beside the bloodied body of Conor Harris. He looked at the ragged ring of people that surrounded them. He heard the word *cops* spoken several times. People were pointing. More people were coming out of the club.

At this point Richard's pulse was elevated and his breathing was harsh and sore.

He remembered that he felt extraordinarily happy. He felt a sudden sense of elated clarity.

He knew they had to get out of there.

He had trouble getting Barry to move. This is the detail that has stuck in many peoples' minds: that Barry was reluctant to leave the side of the boy that a few minutes ago he had been punching and kicking into unconsciousness.

For many people, Barry Fox was the wild card, the boy who shouldn't have been there at all. He was too gentle, said the people who knew him. At Brookfield there was widespread astonishment that Barry Fox, of all people, had been one of the boys involved in Conor Harris's death.

For others, Barry's moment of kindness in the aftermath of the beating could be seen as nothing but hypocrisy.

By themselves, these views are too simplistic, I think. It was entirely characteristic of Barry to kneel beside Conor's fallen body to see how badly he was hurt, to see if there was anything to be done; just as it was characteristic of him to be in Harry's Niteclub in the first place, drinking cheap cider with the Brookfield boys; just as it was characteristic of him to deliver one of the three kicks that knocked Conor out and that ultimately resulted in his death.

17

Because most of the attention during the arrests and the trial focussed on Richard Culhane and his family, I haven't been able to piece together a great deal about the Foxes. But I knew Barry Fox. He was on the famous Senior Cup team that brought home the cup in 2001, the same Senior Cup team that Richard Culhane and Conor Harris were on.

(It's important to remember, by the way, that just because Conor and Richard were on the same rugby team, this didn't mean they were automatically friends. The papers made a lot of the notion that the dead boy and his victim had been teammates. But it didn't work that way. Conor's lingering aura of nouveau-riche unsuitability had always effectively excluded him from the inner circle of Brookfield Senior Cup boys. Conor was on the team, but he wasn't part of the gang. Conor had his own gang, some of whom were on the team, some of whom were not.)

Barry Fox's body was tough and loose. He was built like a chain-link fence. He was, in the words of Father Connelly, 'One hell of a mighty kicker.'

During their Leaving Cert. mock exams, Barry's fifth-year English class was asked to write an essay entitled 'Brookfield'. Barry composed a lyrical description of walking along the avenue to school in the morning, past the blooming beech tree. The essay was graded B minus.

Barry's mother died of breast cancer when Barry was twelve.

Some of the Brookfield first years were taken to the funeral. Barry was missing from school for a lot of that year. When he came back, he seemed not to have changed at all. But there were rumours that he had needed grief counselling to get over the loss.

In the aftermath of Barry's mother's death, Stephen O'Brien's father used to come over to the house to cook meals for Barry and his father. The families had known each other for years.

Barry's father was a cost accountant and his mother, before she died, had been a dental nurse. They had grown up on the same street in Dun Laoghaire. She had died quickly, Barry's mother: three months after the first diagnosis. 'They wanted to send her to Canada,' Barry said. 'There was this new treatment there that would bring about remission in, like, 80 per cent of cases. But she was too sick. We brought her home for the last two weeks. We didn't sleep. Just took care of her. I'd go down to the kitchen at, like, four in the morning and my dad would be there, playing patience with three cups of cold tea in front of him. We both made tea all the time. Fifty cups a day. Never drank any of it, you know. It was just something to do.'

Every now and then, during Barry's time at Brookfield, Father Connelly brought Barry into his office to see how he was getting on. Father Connelly's office overlooked the quad, and Barry would sit looking down at the cobblestones and the flowerboxes underneath the window.

'How are you keeping, Barry? Is everything alright at home?'

'Yeah, everything's okay.'

Father Connelly found that he could get very little out of Barry. The boy was reluctant to talk about anything more significant than how the Junior Cup team were doing. Eventually Father Connelly remembered his counsellor's training and asked Barry about his dreams.

'What do you dream about?'

Barry shrugged. 'The usual stuff, I suppose. Nothing bizarre, like. Girls, and things.'

'Well what did you dream about last night?'

Barry looked at the ceiling. 'Ducks,' he said. 'They flew away. South, like. For the winter.'

'Were you sad to see them go?'

'Yeah.'

'And do you dream often about these ducks?'

'Yeah, most nights, I think.'

'Do you think,' Father Connelly said gently, 'that these ducks might represent your mother?'

'Yeah,' Barry said slowly. 'I think they do.'

Barry told his friends about the ducks, and it became a running joke on poor Father Connelly. Whenever Barry wanted to get out of a test or some homework, he would go into school early in the morning and slip a note under Father Connelly's office door that said, DREAMED ABOUT THE DUCKS AGAIN. Father Connelly would rush to the relevant classroom and bring Barry up to his office for tea and biscuits and a chat.

'Ah, the poor young fella,' Father Connelly said to the other boys. 'It's hard to get by without your mammy.'

Up to a point, Barry made a joke of his mother's death. It was what you did, in a boys' school. The other boys recognized Barry's need to be lighthearted about this subject, and they colluded in his jokey manipulation of Father Connelly and the powers-that-be. Only once did the subject become too serious for Barry to joke about.

We were all at Jesuit schools, of course. (Barry Fox was a Catholic, too.) In fifth year it was customary for the schools to organize retreats at a priory in Athy. Barry and I were in fifth year at the same time, and it happened that my class was on retreat at the priory at the same time as the Brookfield boys.

The priory was an eighteenth-century country home surrounded by forty acres of forested grounds. We arrived in our coaches and spent the first half of the morning getting settled in. This was in October of 2000. We were to stay for three nights – a long weekend. Then there was a Mass, and confession. Meals were scarce; we were expected to dedicate our weekend to fasting and contemplation, and on the Saturday afternoon we were taken on a ten-mile hike up the gentle slope of a nearby hill, which we were expected to complete without our socks and shoes.

I remember being surprised at how seriously the boys took the retreat. Usually they would have been horsing around, swapping stories about girls, throwing spitballs at each other. But they were hushed and thoughtful.

I picked out Barry Fox, on that first afternoon, standing off by himself near the entrance to the chapel while the other boys talked on the lawn in the sun.

That first afternoon we were broken up into groups and taken to dusty seminar rooms with high windows. 'What is this, group therapy?' Dave Whelehan asked, but somebody shushed him. I don't know what you'd call those afternoon sessions: prayer groups, healing encounters. I don't think I ever heard anyone actually call them what they were, which was psychotherapy by other means. Eight or nine of us would sit in a circle and have various discussions chaired by one of the monks of the priory. We were encouraged to talk about things we hadn't talked about before. If the moment seemed right, we were encouraged to cry.

When the weekend was over, we were given little badges to wear. We took them back to Dublin and wore them as though we were Freemasons, a society bound together by the secret sameness of our hearts.

It's possible that Barry Fox was wearing his priory badge on the night he killed Conor Harris. I can't find this out for sure.

Because Barry and I were from different schools, we weren't in the same afternoon session. I heard about what happened to him only later, from one of the boys who had been in Barry's group.

It was the practice of the priory, working with the school, to invite parents to write a letter to their son in which they said various things they would find it difficult to say under normal circumstances. This letter would be sent to the priory and delivered to the boy as a surprise during the last afternoon session.

The letters followed a predictable pattern. Conor Harris's letter said, 'It hasn't always been easy, son, but you know you can always rely on us to see you through.' Richard Culhane's letter said, 'I'll always be there on the sidelines, Richie, cheering you on to even better things.'

Richard's letter had been written by Peter alone. Katherine had refused to have anything to do with it.

Only Peter ever called Richard 'Richie'.

Receiving the letters at the end of the retreat was a moment charged with emotion. Boys cried on each others' shoulders.

'I fucking love my old pair, man,' Conor Harris said, crying on Fergal Morrison's shoulder.

Barry Fox's letter appeared to be from his mother.

The story went around in the week after the retreat. Barry had opened his envelope and read the letter. Although most of the boys in his group were crying, Barry said nothing. He didn't move.

Barry's mother had been dead for almost five years at this point.

We heard afterward that the letter contained references to events that had taken place since Barry's mother's death.

He didn't recognize the handwriting.

It was signed at the end, *All my love, Mum.*

Who wrote the letter? The most logical assumption is that someone at the school wrote it, or someone at the priory. But how had they known enough about Barry's life to sound convincing? Did Barry's father collude in the project? Why had anyone thought it would be a good idea to send Barry a letter that appeared to come from beyond the grave?

According to the boys who were in Barry's group, Barry said nothing for a very long time. The boys took a while to notice that he hadn't joined in the crying and hugging. Then they collected themselves and asked Barry if he was okay.

He didn't say anything. He stood up and left the room.

He walked down the main stairs of the priory and opened the front door. A flock of sparrows cast its sudden script across the sky. Crisp fog rose from the stubbled fields.

Barry walked towards the woods. It was a distance of perhaps three hundred yards. He was still holding the letter in his right hand.

It was late afternoon and it was beginning to get cold.

The boys from Barry's group clustered around the window to watch him, ignoring the protests of the brother who was chairing the session. 'I swear to God,' one of the boys said afterward, 'I thought he was going to top himself. I thought he was going to walk into those woods and we'd find him dangling from a tree a few hours later.'

Barry walked into the woods carrying the letter that purported to be from his mother and didn't come back for an hour. By this time, the priory authorities had alerted the school authorities. Mr Fogarty, the fat biology teacher (who once interrupted a dissection class to point out the window and say in a fluty, high-pitched voice, 'Look! There's a little bird with a worm in its mouth!'), began to organize a search party.

The search party of Brookfield teachers and students was just setting out from the door of the priory when someone spotted Barry emerging from the woods. He no longer seemed to have the letter in his hand. He walked towards the group slowly, without looking up. Nearer the building, his school shoes crunched in the deep gravel.

When they asked him what he'd been doing, he said, 'I just felt like taking a walk.'

What strikes me as odd about this story isn't that no one apologized to Barry for writing a letter that was supposed to be from his dead mother. What strikes me as odd is that nobody in charge during the retreat seemed to know anything about what the letter contained.

Barry said he never asked his father about the letter. His father never mentioned it.

This suggests another possibility for the source of the letter.

It might have been written by another Brookfield boy.

Who else could know enough about Barry's life to convincingly document his recent experiences? Very few other people could have known about the letters-from-parents in advance of the retreat.

But no one ever owned up to having written the letter, and the letter itself seems to have disappeared.

Other questions remain.

What did Barry do while he was alone in the forest for an hour? Did he destroy the letter? Did he think about killing himself, as some people have suggested? Did he simply walk around, wondering what had happened, and why?

I have no access to Barry Fox's mind or memory. At the trial, his testimony was the most clipped, the most uninformative. But I've always seen in him a depth I don't see in Stephen O'Brien or even in Richard Culhane.

Perhaps this is because I was standing by the door of the priory, with a small group of Merrion Academy boys, when Barry emerged from the woods. I saw him walk slowly back towards the building across the long stretch of darkening grass, his shoulders low and his hands in his pockets, a look of tense introspection on his pale and pudgy face.

Was this how he looked as he knelt beside Conor Harris and leaned in to see if the boy he'd attacked was still breathing?

Barry was the one who thought about things.

Or so I've found myself believing.

18

When it came to the Dublin girls' schools, you knew that each of them would produce a slightly different kind of girl. Girls from different schools dressed differently, used different slang, went out with different kinds of boy. The differences were miniscule, of course, but if you were practised, you could guess which school a girl had gone to after five minutes of ordinary conversation. Ailesbury College girls were burnished and vain. They did things like ballet and lacrosse. St Anne's girls – if they were blonde – were cutters, or – if they weren't blonde – were fat and paranoid and smoked a lot. St Anne's girls (it was generally and erroneously believed) would sleep with almost anyone. (Once I heard someone suggest that the school motto for St Anne's College, Foxrock, should be, 'I'm With the Band'.) St Brigid's girls joined committees and, when they got to university, they ran for class president. Elm Park girls were a lot like Ailesbury College girls, but they had (it was whispered) more sex.

Of course the girls who went to these schools had many things in common. They watched the same American soaps and they listened to the same bands and they went to the same clubs. To ascertain the differences, you had to be on the inside. You had to be part of that world.

The boys' schools weren't so easily distinguishable. There wasn't much difference, in other words, between a boy who'd gone to Brookfield and a boy who'd gone to Michael's or a boy who'd gone to Blackrock or Merrion. If you'd gone to any of these schools you played rugby or soccer and you wore Gap chinos that you'd bought when you were in the States and Ben Sherman shirts and Jack Jones hoodies. You wore Nike trainers that cost two hundred euro. You probably had a car and you drank Stella or Dutch Gold or Bulmers and when you were drunk you sang either 'Livin' on a Prayer' or 'My Way' with your arms around your friends.

I once saw Richard Culhane sing 'My Way' with his arms around a circle of Brookfield boys. This was in the ballroom of the Shelbourne Hotel in the waning hours of a university black-tie ball. There were balloons and wilted streamers on the spotlit dance floor, and tired girls at empty tables. As the song ended the Brookfield boys started doing high kicks, like a chorus line. They were the last to leave.

19

What none of them knew – not even Richard, although he found out after his arrest – was that Laura was seeing a counsellor. Her parents sent her to 'a woman they trusted' in the aftermath of Laura's grandmother's death, when Laura 'just didn't seem to be getting back on track'; but in reality Laura had been wandering in and out of depressions for years. She had an eating disorder too, a mild form of anorexia that meant she would refuse to eat for days at a time. She would sit and smile at the family dinner table, swallow a few tiny mouthfuls, and artfully move the rest of her food around her plate to give the impression that she had eaten almost all of it. Then she would make sure to scrape it into the bin before her mother got a closer look.

Laura's depressions had started in her early teens. When she was thirteen the family dog died of stomach cancer, and Laura, who had walked the dog every afternoon in the fields behind the house, was inconsolable. This was the summer holidays, and now she had nothing to do. She began to drift around the house in her pyjamas. Laura's mother was seldom home, and when she was in the house she spent most of her time on the phone, helping to arrange her sister's wedding.

One morning Laura wandered out into the garden. She looked at the three-foot fence her father had built around the kennel to give the dog some room to play in so he wouldn't damage the flowerbeds.

Laura went down to the garden shed and found a tin of white paint and a stiff-bristled brush. She began painting the dog's fence, from left to right, covering the unvarnished wood in a layer of matt white. The brush was old and the going was hard. When the first coat was dry she started again. The whole job took her until late afternoon.

When she was finished and the second coat was dry, she kicked the fence down, methodically, plank by plank.

'What's she doing out there?' her father asked, when he came home from work and went to the kitchen window.

'Don't disturb her,' Laura's mother said. 'At least she's keeping herself occupied.'

Laura's counsellor's name was Dr Alison Reid, and Laura's father had known her at university. As far as I've been able to find out, Laura liked her, even preferred her to her parents as an outlet for anxiety and pain. The newspapers didn't find out about Dr Reid until the trial was almost over. One morning in October Dr Reid turned up at her office in a Victorian terrace in Ranelagh to find cameramen and journalists arrayed outside. She refused to talk to them, though her friendship with the Haines family gave rise to a couple of articles about what the media had taken to calling 'the old boys' network', as if Dr Reid were simply the latest member of a countrywide conspiracy to be unmasked as the true evil behind Conor Harris's death.

Laura went to see Dr Reid every Tuesday afternoon.

'And how are we feeling this week, Laura?' Dr Reid would ask.

'Fine,' Laura said.

'How do you feel about food at the moment?'

'Alright, I suppose.'

'Are you eating?'

'Two meals a day. But I exercise, so that gets rid of it.'

'We've talked about the importance of a healthy balance between food and exercise, haven't we, Laura?'

'I suppose so.'

'And how's Conor doing?'

'He's good. He, like, keeps an eye on what I eat.'

'And how does that make you feel?'

'Like he loves me, I suppose.'

'But?'

'But … it also kind of pisses me off. Like, what does he care what I eat? What fucking business is it of his?'

'If he loves you, he wants you to be healthy. It's probably important to him.'

'Yeah.'

'Do you think Conor loves you?'

'Yeah. I suppose he does.'

'And how does that make you feel?'

'You always want to know that. You always want to know how things make me feel.'

'Isn't that what we're here to talk about? How things make you feel?'

'Yeah, but it's just, like, what is that, some mantra you learned in therapy school?'

'Do you think you're trying to avoid my question, Laura?'

'No.'

'You suppose Conor loves you. How does that make you feel?'

'Honestly?'

'Of course.'

'It kind of, like, annoys me a little bit. He's like this puppy. You know the way, sometimes people are so, like, *vulnerable*, and it just makes you want to, like, kick them?'

'Does Conor make you feel that way?'

'Not really. Only sometimes. He's got this way of looking at me, like when I tell him I don't want to eat or something, like it's all his fault, like he mustn't be good enough for me if I don't want to eat to keep him happy. But it's not *about* him. I keep telling him that. It hasn't got anything to do with him.'

'Do you think he really feels that way?'

'I don't know,' Laura said. 'I don't know how anyone feels.'

I heard Laura speak these words, *I don't know how anyone feels*, at a party in Conor Harris's house, a year before Richard was arrested. I think she was telling the truth. I think Laura's chief failure, in all of this, has been a failure of empathy, a failure to intuit how other people felt – about her, about Richard, about Conor Harris and how he died.

At the end of every fourth session, Dr Reid would write Laura a prescription for a month's supply of Lexapro. She had taken one of these pills – a popular antidepressant – the night Conor died. Coincidentally, Lexapro was the drug prescibed to Eileen Harris to help her deal with the difficulties of Richard's cancelled manslaughter trial. But that was two years later, and by then everything had changed.

20

When she was thirteen years old Laura Haines asked her mother if she could get her ears pierced. All the girls in her Ailesbury College class were doing it, she said. Mary Haines brought Laura to the pharmacy in Blackrock, and Laura twitched and winced as the pharmacist jabbed at her earlobes. The pharmacist smelled like the sweet barley sticks Mary always bought for Laura after a visit to the doctor. The piercings swelled up almost immediately, and Laura complained until Mary, in desperation, bought two ice pops to cool the swelling, and Laura followed her mother home with the ice pops pressed to her temples, waiting till her ears turned numb.

I've heard Laura Haines described (usually by women, in confidential tones) as 'superficial'. I'm not sure what this means, aside from connoting a general preoccupation with appearances, with the aesthetic surface of things. I believe it would be a mistake to think of Laura as obsessed with trivialities. But people were misled by the amount of attention she paid to how she looked and how she lived.

It's worth recording the material aspects of Laura's life. In this as in so many other things, she is almost representative – as representative as any individual, with all the usual peculiarities of selfhood, can ever be.

Every ten days or so Laura spent a hundred and ninety euro at a salon in Ranelagh called Sun Worship Tanning. Here she would lie for half an hour in a coffin-shaped plastic box, soaking up the artificial sunlight. Some girls did this naked, but Laura always wore the bottom half of a bikini, with the result (according to Conor) that her ass was always marked out with a pale trapezoid of untanned skin.

Laura would only get her hair done at certain hairdressers'. She would only shop at certain boutiques. When she was fifteen she asked a friend of her father's if he had ever been to the Dundrum Town Centre. When he said he hadn't, Laura said, 'My *God*, you haven't *lived*.' The family laughed about this, but Laura had been utterly serious.

She bought a new mobile phone every six months. Her favourite was a microscopic Japanese camera-phone with a baby-pink casing.

She bought earrings and necklaces and bracelets and forgot about them. Her bedroom was generally pristine – white walls and bare boards, stuffed animals in precise ranks – but her walk-in wardrobe was a chaos of discarded jewellery and clothes worn only once.

Laura dressed in a way that anyone raised in south County Dublin during those years would have found immediately recognizable. 'Essential elements of this uniform' – I quote now from *The Irish Times*, 1 December 2007 – 'are a ladies'-fit Leinster jersey (€49.99) and palomino pony Ugg boots (€249), both from Arnotts.'

Every September Laura went to Paris with her mother to shop for clothes they couldn't get in Dublin.

She ordered American Eagle hoodies and Abercrombie sweatpants over the web. In winter she wore a scarf by DKNY.

Laura and her friends had various names for people who had less money than they did, or who had not been able to go to private schools. They called them 'povvos' or 'knackers' or 'chavs' or 'skobes'. Distinctions of dress were frequently made. Pink tracksuit bottoms by themselves did not make you look like a skobe. But pink tracksuit bottoms with a pink tracksuit top certainly did. These distinctions were rigorously policed. Laura was one of the people who did the policing.

Girls who wanted to know what to wear consulted Laura Haines's Bebo page. Laura would say: 'I wish I was as thin as Mischa Barton.' Other girls would say, 'I wish I was as thin as Laura Haines.'

Laura bought perfume by Prada and deodorant by Ralph Lauren.

It's tempting to regard these things as added extras. But really they were fundamental. They were *sine qua non*.

21

In school we used to tell a joke about the difference between Irish people and American people.

An American drives past an enormous house on a hill. The American sees a swimming pool and a heated jacuzzi and a sports car and an SUV and a landscaped garden. He sees stables out back. And he sees the man who owns all this, standing on his front porch, holding hands with his beautiful wife and watching the sun go down on his vast estate.

The American shakes his head and thinks, *One day, I'm gonna be just like him.*

Five minutes later an Irishman drives by the same house. He sees the swimming pool and the heated jacuzzi and the sports car and the SUV and the landscaped garden. He sees the stables out back. He sees the man and his beautiful wife, watching the sun go down.

The Irishman shakes his head and thinks, *One day, I'm gonna get that bastard.*

22

Stephen O'Brien used to boast that he had fucked at least one girl from each of the Dublin private girls' schools. 'I'm missing Mount Anville, man,' he would complain to the Brookfield boys. On nights out in Russell's or the Wicked Wolf Stephen would tell his friends to prowl the dance floor in search of a Mountie, and to let him know if they found one.

If he was known as a swordsman, it was in the affectionate, even condescending way that people reserve for a man they don't entirely trust. No one ever quite knew whether to believe Stephen's stories about his conquests. The stories were too unverifiable, too problematically private.

'Met this girl at a tutorial last week,' he would say. 'Went for coffee. Bam, twenty minutes later she was sucking my cock in the toilets beside Dramsoc.'

'The O'Brien strikes again!' Barry Fox would shout.

The boys would high-five.

The problem with these stories was that they might just have happened. And Stephen was a good-looking guy. He wasn't as universally adored as Richard Culhane, but on nights out he would score almost as often. Like Conor Harris, he had a penchant for scoring other peoples' girlfriends. But Stephen made a point of it. He said he was doing it just to be a cunt.

Stephen was the first Brookfield boy in his class to lose his virginity. It happened one night after the Wesley Disco, in the back seat of Maurice O'Brien's BMW, which was parked in the driveway of the O'Briens' house at the time. Stephen had taken a St Anne's girl named Ailbhe Connor home in a cab. Seeking proof that this story was true, Barry Fox and Richard Culhane drove over to Ailbhe Connor's house the next afternoon and asked her about it.

She told them the story was true but that Stephen O'Brien hadn't been her first time.

This was when Stephen O'Brien was in his fifth year at Brookfield. He was at that stage of teenage boyhood where blushes come unbidden at the faintest innuendo, the tiniest mistake. But when Steve told the story of how he had lost his virginity, he didn't blush.

For his Leaving Cert. year Stephen transferred to Merrion Academy because a place had opened up and Maurice O'Brien, a Merrion boy, wanted Stephen to graduate from the same school that he had gone to.

What Stephen O'Brien really wanted was a steady girlfriend. Like almost everyone else at Brookfield, he believed in a chivalric code of commitment and respect. And like all misogynists, he was sentimental about women.

Private schools depend for their continued existence on the inculcation of a conservative sentimentality in their pupils. Settle down with the girl of your dreams, stay happy, stay faithful.

Semper et Ubique Fidelis.

Stephen's first girlfriend was a St Brigid's girl named Aisling Kelly. St Brigid's, Killiney, was famous for its businesslike traditionalism, and the girls were famous for their virtue. This, I think, was what appealed to Stephen O'Brien about his first serious girlfriend.

The first time I met Aisling Kelly she was wearing an old-womanish cardigan, mossy-green and fastened with oversized plastic buttons, and a skirt tied with a broad leather belt. She was carrying her folder of school notes, each section alphabetized and tagged with green or pink labels.

'What do you think will come up on Biology Paper Two?' she asked me.

Stephen broke up with her after two months.

'Did you fuck her, man?' Fergal Morrison asked him, two weeks later, voicing the question that was on everybody's mind.

Stephen silently held up his hand for the high five.

Two weeks after they had broken up, Stephen sent Aisling a text message that said, GUESS WHO I GOT A BLOWJOB FROM LAST NITE? HINT, IT WASNT U!!!!

A fact about Stephen O'Brien that never made it into any of the newspapers: he was worried about losing his hair. Maurice O'Brien was bald except for a coin of scalp showing at his tufted crown. Stephen's hairline was receding noticeably by the time he was eighteen. It was something he mentioned only to his closest friends, and only in moments of real intimacy.

You didn't slag Stephen O'Brien about his hair. It just wasn't done.

Stephen didn't look like a violent man. He looked like a *strong* man – you took his strength for granted. But you wouldn't have marked him for a killer.

A few days after Stephen had broken up with her, Aisling Kelly complained to her friends that Stephen didn't know how to put a condom on correctly. 'He doesn't pinch the little bit at the top. You know what I mean? He just, like, rolls it on. There was no fucking way I was getting an abortion for Stephen O'Fucking Brien. So I told him to cop on and leave me alone.'

People began to say that it was Aisling who had broken up with Steve, instead of the other way around. Nobody at Brookfield believed these rumours.

Maurice and Kitty O'Brien were the prosperous children of, respectively, a doctor and a lawyer. Trinity-educated as undergraduates – two years apart – they had met when they were both pursuing graduate degrees in Business Administration at Oxford. They owned a three-story house in Ranelagh that they had bought and fixed up in the late 1970s. Maurice was a senior executive in the Irish branch of an international software development company. Kitty owned and operated a beauty salon in Donnybrook. Eileen Harris and Katherine Culhane regularly went to this beauty salon, where Kitty O'Brien gave them a discount.

Is it significant, I wonder, that all three boys who went to prison for killing Conor Harris were only children? Does it make a difference?

Historically, of course, the middle classes have always had fewer children than any other class. But these were Catholic families – Irish families. Why did the Culhanes, the O'Briens, and the Foxes not produce more than one child each? Was this a contributing factor to what happened on the last night of summer, 2004?

In trying to make sense of the events of this single night, the night that Conor died, I find myself drawn into deeper and deeper mysteries: mysteries of character, mysteries of influence, mysteries of motivation. These are questions nobody can answer. But I'd like an answer to them, even so.

On New Year's Eve, 2003, Barry Fox threw a party. This was the party at which Barry and Stephen O'Brien almost fell out.

It was unusual for Stephen to have been invited at all. Barry's New Year's parties were, usually, Brookfield occasions. But Stephen was going out with a new girl by then – Clodagh Finnegan, his long-term girlfriend, who was there on the night Conor died – and she was the sister of Andy Finnegan, who had played scrum half for the Brookfield SCT.

Stephen had met Clodagh at the UCD Fresher's Ball in September, 2003. Stephen was a second year by then, but going to the Fresher's Ball was still de rigueur for all Quinn School students and former Brookfield boys. Clodagh was a St Anne's girl who wore hoodies and short ruffled skirts and no tights. She had an overlong lopsided fringe that made her tilt her head back so she could see you. Stephen O'Brien was in love with her, I think. It wasn't obvious, because Steve was undemonstrative, except when he was drunk, but I always thought that he and Clodagh would last. They were the kind of couple you quickly learn to take for granted.

Clodagh broke up with Steve when she found out he'd been involved in Conor's death.

What Stephen liked about Clodagh was that she liked sex as much as he did. 'She lets me put it anywhere I *want*, man,' he told Richard Culhane.

'That's, like … way too much information, Steve,' Richard said.

The only problem with Clodagh was that she drove Stephen's friends crazy.

'That girl fucking *never* stops talking,' Barry Fox complained to me once.

The guys would sit in Eddie Rocket's listening as Clodagh talked to Steve.

'You don't understand, Steve, she's being *such* a bitch,' Clodagh said. 'So she comes over to my till and she's like, *Clodagh*, have you see the roster cos your name is down for Saturday and you have to make sure you get the right time and blah blah blah. So I'm there, Yeah, yeah, it's cool and blah blah blah. But then OMIGOD I love this song have you heard this it's AMAZING, it's *so* about me and Michael. Just imagine: this song, car, country road, spliff. D'you know what I mean? So I'm like, *why* are you being such a *bitch* about this, you're only doing it because Daniel said he'd let me take a smoke break half an hour early and Steve, she *so* wants to fuck him it's unbelievable. So I was out there, like, having my smoke break and did you order chilli fries? Did I? I ordered the milkshake.'

The adult world – the world of social and moral subtlety in which everyone else was gradually finding their way – was something that flickered at the edges of Clodagh's attention. If she saw it, she never saw it whole; she saw the parts that related to herself, and these she commandeered as material for her endless chatter.

Steve would sit in stoic silence, nodding at the proper moments, listening to every word.

On the night Conor died Clodagh was in the taxi that Richard Culhane, Laura Haines, and Stephen O'Brien took home. Richard and Laura were silent for the whole journey. Stephen and Clodagh talked about the fight, all the way to Richard's house.

The next afternoon their taxi driver called the guards. But the guards already knew Conor was dead. It would take them three more weeks to identify the four people who had taken that taxi home.

Conor Harris wasn't at Barry's Fox's 2003 New Year's Eve party. He was at a smaller party in Laura Haines's parents' house.

Barry threw the party in his grandfather's summer house in Wexford. Thirty-five people drove down on New Year's Eve. They weren't particularly impressed by the house. The walls were mildewed and the bedrooms were cold. Propped in the shower was the lopsided shell of a plastic canoe. The house was by the shore, and a short tongue of lawn protruded as if to lap at the incoming sea. Barry's grandfather had built the house in the late sixties and it hadn't been renovated since.

'Barry,' Stephen O'Brien shouted as he toured the house, 'is it alright if we trash the place, like?'

Barry got everybody together in the living room and said, 'Alright, guys, it's grand if you go a bit mental, like. There's only one thing I'll ask you to do, right? My parents are coming down here next weekend, so keep the bedroom at the end of the hall clear for the night, 'cos that's their room. Okay?'

Everyone said that was fine.

To make sure, Barry locked his parents' bedroom door.

The party rapidly got out of hand. Fergal Morrison set up a beer-bong in the kitchen doorway, and every few minutes someone would lie underneath it while someone else filled the funnel. Somebody started a small bonfire in the back garden. Dave Whelehan sat at the living-room coffee table and rolled spliffs. Everyone was dancing and drinking. A game of soggy biscuit developed in one of the bedrooms. People were playing poker on the bathroom floor. People were playing Kings or Truth or Dare. People were arm-wrestling at the kitchen table. Somebody threw up on a houseplant in the hall. The canoe was taken from the shower cubicle and set up in the front garden. By the end of the night the canoe was on top of Richard Culhane's car.

Richard spent most of the night talking to a Mount Anville girl named Kate Kerrigan. He kept touching the back of his head with his left palm. Kate kept touching Richard's nose and laughing.

Fergal Morrison threw up in the kitchen sink.

Once the countdown was over and it was officially 2004, the year in which Conor Harris would die, the party began to calm down.

Stephen O'Brien had spent the two hours leading up to the count-down kissing Clodagh Finnegan on the living-room couch. Clodagh said she wanted to be wherever the joints were being rolled. Stephen didn't smoke hash, but he was happy to sit on the couch with Clodagh on his knee and his hand up her skirt. She was wearing a thong and it was easy for him to get a finger or two inside her pussy.

By this stage Stephen had almost finished a case of Stella and half a bottle of vodka. Clodagh was drinking bottles of alcoholic lemonade.

Eventually Clodagh whispered in Stephen's ear, 'So are you going to fuck me or what?'

They looked around for an empty bedroom. There weren't any. Both of the bathrooms were occupied.

Stephen found the locked door at the end of the corridor, and shouldered it open.

He and Clodagh had sex on Barry's parents' bed.

In the kitchen Barry looked around and said, 'Where's Steve and Clodagh?'

He looked around. Then he went into his parents' bedroom.

'Aw, what the *fuck*?' Barry shouted. 'The one thing I asked you, Steve. The one *fucking* thing I asked you!'

The lock on the door was broken and the wood around it was splintered. Clodagh and Steve had finished by this point. Steve had put his jeans back on. Clodagh, still naked, hid beneath the covers.

'Relax, man,' Steve said. 'Take a fucking chill pill, or whatever. I'll pay for a new lock, like.'

'That's not the point, man,' Barry said. He was on the verge of tears. 'This was the *only* fucking thing I asked you not to do and you went ahead and did it. You're *such* a fucking geebag, Steve.'

'Sorry, Barry,' Clodagh said in a small voice.

'Here, fuck off, man,' Steve said. He put his T-shirt on. 'I didn't know, alright?'

'That's such fucking bollocks, man. Get the fuck out of my house. You're such a fucking cunt.'

'You can't fucking throw me out.' Steve was starting to laugh. 'We're in the arsehole of fucking nowhere, like. Where the fuck am I supposed to go?'

'Just get the fuck out. And take that stupid bitch with you, alright?'

Steve was standing very close to Barry. They were both tall but Stephen was slightly taller.

'Get ... the fuck ... out,' Barry said.

'Don't be a prick about it,' Steve said. He had stopped laughing.

Barry walked away, back towards the kitchen. 'I'm calling the guards,' he said.

A crowd had gathered. Steve, his pride stung, went after Barry. 'Relax, man, for fuck's sake. I'll even get Clodagh to like, wash the sheets and stuff. We didn't do anything weird, I just like, fucked her, or whatever.'

'You fucking disrespectful cunt,' Barry said.

'Fuck you, man,' Steve said.

Barry stood with his back to Steve. He had taken out his mobile phone and begun to dial.

Steve picked up a wine glass from the top of the fridge and threw it at the floor.

'That's what I think of your fucking house, man,' he said.

Barry dropped his phone and charged at Steve. They both got in a couple of punches before they were broken up by, among others, Richard Culhane.

'It's not worth it,' Richard kept shouting, 'It's not worth it.'

Steve's nose was bleeding. Richard took him out into the front garden to calm him down.

Barry paced up and down the kitchen saying, '*Fuck*.'

In the garden Steve dabbed at his nose with a paper napkin and snorted and grimaced. 'What the fuck, Richard?'

'You shouldn't have fucked your girlfriend in his parents' bed, man,' Richard said.

'How the fuck was I supposed to know it was his parents' bed? He's *SUCH A CUNT*!'

Steve kicked at a flowerpot. It broke with a dull, earthy shatter.

Barry arrived at the door. 'What the fuck are you doing?'

'Fuck you!' Steve said.

'Get the fuck out of my house, you bald little cunt,' Barry said.

Steve picked up another flowerpot and put it through the wind-screen of Barry's car.

You didn't slag Stephen O'Brien about his hair.

Somehow, Richard Culhane calmed the situation down. He was usually able to do this. His was always the voice of reason, the voice of moderation. He convinced Stephen to pay for a replacement windscreen. He convinced him to apologize for having sex in Barry's parents' bed. He convinced Barry to let Steve and Clodagh stay at the party, since they had nowhere else to go. He convinced Barry to apologize to Clodagh for calling her a bitch.

'You're such a hero,' Clodagh told Richard. 'Seriously.' To Barry she said, 'Sorry to cause so much D-R-A-M-A at your party, like.'

She spelled it out: D-R-A-M-A.

Bang.

Bang.

Bang.

PART TWO

La Belle Epoque

23

We all went to Conor's funeral. Because of the need for an autopsy, it wasn't held until almost two weeks after the night he died. The weather was astonishing: blue skies and pewter sunlight. Mourners sweated in their sombre clothes. The funeral was a media event, although Eileen and Brendan Harris had done all they could to prevent this from happening. It was also a rugby funeral: the Church of the Sacred Heart in Donnybrook was packed with the Senior Cup teams from five Dublin schools, along with their friends, families, girlfriends and former coaches. Some of the players from the Ireland squad were there. Conor's teachers from Brookfield sat up front. There were golfing friends of Brendan Harris's and women from Eileen Harris's Thursday quilting workshop. The staff of the four restaurants owned by the Harrises were there. Maurice O'Brien and his wife and Barry's father, Gerard Fox, were there. Peter and Katherine Culhane sat somewhere in the middle. It was rumoured, later, that Gerald Clinch, Peter Culhane's solicitor, had been at Conor's funeral, but I didn't see him on the day, nor would I have known what he looked like at that point, before his picture had appeared in the papers.

Laura Haines was there, sitting towards the back with her mother and father, wearing sunglasses to hide the puffiness of her eyes.

The Brookfield colours were much in evidence. Conor's coffin was draped in a Brookfield jersey as it was borne down the aisle at the end of the service. Eileen hadn't wanted this, but Brendan had said, 'It was a part of who he was. And people will expect it.'

'We're not doing this for other people,' Eileen said.

'Yes we are,' Brendan said.

He meant a great deal by this remark. He meant that Conor's funeral would not just be an opportunity to mourn. It would also be an opportunity for the Harrises to show how deeply angry they were, how committed they were to finding justice for their murdered son.

He also meant that funerals had always seemed to him the occasions of a needless public martyrdom. He wanted to grieve in private. But the world wouldn't let him.

'He was murdered, Eileen,' Brendan kept insisting. 'I don't care what anyone says. Our boy was murdered.'

Each time he said this, Brendan seemed to find new impetus for his anger.

If you don't have real strength, he had learned, anger will often suffice.

The night before the funeral, Brendan had wheeled out the recycling bin and set it on the kerb. He wanted to keep busy. He wanted to immerse himself in the domestic, the housebound. Standing in the driveway, he looked around at the neighbouring houses, at the dormant, shiny cars. He saw the small red security lights that ticked on the dashboards of the jeeps and SUVs.

Security, he thought. *We've lost it, now. We are no longer secure.*

Newspaper reporters and TV crews had been asked to stay outside the church, but during the Mass there were occasional flares as someone took a picture. I had expected the day to have an air of celebration about it, a sense of novelty perhaps, but the scrutiny of so many strangers, the intrusion of so many into what should have been a private event, seemed to make everyone more grave and solitary. It was a heavy occasion: the warm air was heavy, and people walked heavily as they made their way to the church.

The funeral made the six o'clock news as part of the coverage of the ongoing investigation into Conor's death. There was a stylized solemnity to the image of his coffin being carried out of the church by six pale, shaven college boys, their heads bowed, their eyes lowered. *He was one of us,* their faces seemed to say. *We take care of our own, even in death.* Many people found this the most difficult part of the day. The image showed up on TV every evening for a week.

At this point the gardaí were working on the theory that a rugby-school rivalry had been the cause of the fight that killed Conor.

The church, crammed to overflowing, was stuffy and hot. The Harrises sat in the row nearest the front. Close behind them was their extended family: brothers and cousins, nieces and nephews, aunts and uncles. Directly behind the extended family were Conor's Brookfield Leaving Cert. class, wearing dark suits and red-and-white scarves, respectfully tied. The boys looked unnaturally sombre, sitting in silent ranks on the wooden pews. It was, I suppose, a class reunion of sorts for them, but they had grown up to be sharply conscious of the need to suppress their natural levity at times of crisis such as this.

In the front row of Brookfield boys, Richard Culhane sat without speaking.

Eileen and Brendan Harris were barely conscious of the size and scale of Conor's funeral. The two weeks between their discovery that Conor had been killed and the September morning when they were allowed to bury him seemed, to them, to have been whiled away in a torpid atmosphere of pervasive unreality. During this time they had appeared briefly on television. They had talked exhaustively to the guards about the last time they had spoken to Conor (on his mobile phone, a few minutes before he entered Harry's Niteclub, when he had seemed completely normal, they insisted, completely calm). They had spoken in private to the parish priest. They had shuttled back and forth between their house in Donnybrook and St Vincent's Hospital, waiting to hear when Conor's body would be released. The state pathologist had been in Limerick, performing a post-mortem on the victim of a gangland shooting, and had been unable to get back to Dublin until four days after Conor had died. Even when he arrived and began to examine Conor's body, it became clear that his investigation would take a long time. Conor had been quite badly beaten, he told the gardaí in confidence (this was later leaked to the papers). It would take time to ascertain the cause of death.

'This can't be happening,' Eileen Harris kept saying. 'This can't be happening.'

I remember everyone saying that they expected Eileen Harris to go to pieces in the aftermath of Conor's death. People kept saying this right through the arrests and the trial. But although she was superficially nervy, she was every bit as angry as her husband, and it seemed to give her the strength to go on.

Waiting for the pathologist's report had made the Harrises angry. But this, of course, was just the beginning.

As it happened, the pathologist turned in his report on the morning of Conor's funeral. This was the lead story on the six o'clock news, to which the story of the funeral appeared as an appendix.

What made the funeral worse was that nobody had yet come forward with information about Conor's death.

Brendan and Eileen Harris sat at the front of the church without their son. I remember finding it odd that, instead of sitting between his parents, Conor was lying in a wooden box draped with a Brookfield jersey, a couple of feet in front of them.

I looked at the Harrises. I had never seen two people look so sundered, so fiercely apart.

They hadn't cleaned out Conor's room yet. They hadn't even been able to go into it. Conor's room, where he kept his Brookfield rugby kit and his surprisingly innocuous collection of pornography (just tits and asses, some girl-on-girl videos, the occasional shot of a splayed pussy), and where he kept the red plastic flower he had taken from Laura Haines's hair on cup final day in 2003.

The service began.

The priest (what was his name? although I was there, I was in the church that day, I find I can't remember) began by saying what a terrible loss Conor's family had suffered. He said this loss would be felt keenly, too, by Conor's school and college friends, by his teachers and teammates.

He condemned Ireland's culture of binge-drinking, which he believed had been responsible for Conor's death.

He said, 'Young people think life is cheap. Well, life is not cheap, and we are coming to terms with that terrible truth now.'

He said what a loss Conor's death meant for the game of rugby.

When the priest had finished speaking, Conor's uncle – Eileen's brother – went to the lectern and read an A.E. Housman poem, 'To an Athlete, Dying Young', of which I could recall, when I sat down to write this, only a single stanza:

> Eyes the shady night has shut
> Cannot see the record cut,
> And silence sounds no worse than cheers
> After earth has stopped the ears.

There is another verse, which I have just located in my library copy of *A Shropshire Lad*, that it seems I should have noticed on the day of the funeral, should have spotted and remembered. It goes like this:

> Now you will not swell the rout
> Of lads that wore their honours out,
> Runners whom renown outran
> And the name died before the man.

I think of these lines quite often, now. In the church that day, very few of us were in the mood for poetry. Very few of us were in the mood for anything at all.

Naomi Frears – where had she been, all this time? – read from the Gospel.

The choir sang the 'In Paradisum' from Faure's *Requiem*.

Then Brendan Harris rose to speak about his son.

'My son was murdered,' he said. 'He was beaten to death in cold blood by hooligans when he should have been making his way safely home. My wife and I want to see justice done. We want to see the people who are responsible for this terrible crime punished. We want the balance to be set right. We appreciate the sympathy and understanding we've been shown by so many over the last two weeks. Thank you to everyone who has helped us …' he stopped, and I expected him to cry, but his anger seemed to grow in strength, '… at this difficult time.' His eyes were bright and his hands were in fists. He didn't sound like a man thanking the congregation for its sympathy. He sounded like a judge handing down a death sentence.

If I had known then what we all know now, I would have turned to look at Richard Culhane as Brendan spoke those words. But, like almost everyone else in that sweltering church, I knew nothing. I was, perforce, as ignorant as the rest of them.

I remember wondering, during the service, whether Conor and Laura had ever had sex. He had slept with Naomi Frears, I knew. They had make-up sex the morning after the incident at the Brookfield Debs. But with Laura, you never knew. When we were in sixth year somebody started a rumour that Laura Haines was so attached to her virginity that she would only have anal sex, preserving her pussy for the man she would marry. This was the kind of selflessly destructive rumour perpetrated by the girls in Laura's set. Nobody I knew of took it seriously. Laura was choosy about the men she slept with, yes. But shouldn't we admire this? Shouldn't we tell her that she did a good thing, that sexual continence is one of the truest, the most heartbreaking, of the virtues we have lost?

Nevertheless, I was tolerably sure that Conor had fucked her. You don't fall that deeply in love with someone you aren't fucking.

When Brendan Harris had finished speaking, and made his way in hollow silence to his seat beside his wife, the priest stood and offered Mass.

'Take this, all of you, and eat it,' he said. 'This is my body, which I have given up for you.'

Bang. Bang. Bang.

We fucking showed that little cunt.

Among the people who received communion were Richard Culhane and Barry Fox. They shuffled to the foot of the altar with the rest of the old Senior Cup team.

Perhaps tellingly, perhaps not, Stephen O'Brien elected to remain seated during the Mass. He sat at the back, among the Merrion Park boys. He too wore sunglasses. He didn't take them off during the service.

When the Mass was over, Pat Kilroy stood to speak.

Pat Kilroy was the principal of Brookfield College. He had been the coach of the Senior Cup team for nearly ten years. He had coached them to the 2002 victory over Michael's. He knew Conor Harris and

Richard Culhane and Barry Fox as though they were his sons.

Pat Kilroy had asked the Harrises if he could speak at Conor's funeral. Eileen said no. Brendan said yes.

Pat Kilroy ('Mr Kilroy' to generations of rank-and-file Brookfield students, 'Pat' to parents and to the boys on the SCT) stood at the lectern and looked down at the congregation with the sides of his mouth lowered in a clownish moue. He wore a black suit, and a tie in the Brookfield colours. He was losing the hair above his forehead in triangular notches. He was a Clare man in his fifties, and he had the reckless stance of the teacher who is used to being obeyed, the comfortable slouch, the confident hands.

Mr Kilroy's was a relaxed authority, I've heard. Most of the time he was genial and proud, two qualities, according to the boys, deserving of respect and admiration. 'But you don't want to piss him off,' Barry Fox said once. 'You just don't want him as an enemy, like.'

Pat Kilroy stood at the gleaming lectern. People coughed and whispered.

'We were all,' he began, 'deeply saddened when we heard of Conor's death.' He cleared his throat. 'Saddened for his parents, first of all. But saddened for ourselves, too. Saddened, because we recognized that Brookfield – and by extension, the country – had lost one of its great players. Not a potentially great player. But the real, achieved thing, never mind his youth and his lack of professional experience. Conor wasn't one of those boys who went on to play for the university when his time came to leave us. But I think we all expected him to return to the game at some point, to relive past glories and to attain to new ones.'

He cleared his throat again. He leaned on the lectern with peremptory gusto, but his voice rasped humidly with trapped phlegm.

'As you all know,' he said, 'rugby is very much a part of our way of life at Brookfield. And during Conor's time at the school, I think I could have found no greater example of a student who took that way of life to heart than Conor Harris.'

I remember thinking, *What about Richard Culhane?* And I know that half the people around me were thinking the same thing.

'In his dedication,' Pat Kilroy said, 'his sportsmanship, his courtesy on and off the pitch, his drive and commitment, Conor Harris was an example to us all.'

I was still thinking about Richard Culhane. What I thought was this: *What you're saying would be true if it was Richard who had died.*

At the trial it was established – legally, officially – that Richard had contributed to the Blackrock fracas only at the end, when he delivered his valedictory kick to Conor's head. Privately, people have assured me that this was not the case. When the fight began, Richard was punching just like the rest of them. He had been there at the start of the fight and he was there, flailing indiscriminately, at the very end.

In a sense, of course, it *was* Richard who had died. We just didn't know it yet.

But he did. And so did Pat Kilroy.

When the funeral was over everybody shook hands with the Harrises and went outside to stand on the steps of the church. It was Indian summer on the open streets. There was a tang of salt in the tidal breeze.

'Such a beautiful day,' someone said.

I stood by the doors of the church and watched the people as they talked. At the edges of the crowd, over by the churchyard gates, the television crews pointed their carapaced machines.

I was still thinking about what Pat Kilroy had said at the end of the service. His description of Conor's 'dedication and sportsmanship' squared so poorly with my own memories of Conor's fitful intensity and quarrelsome playing that I felt aggrieved. I wanted people to know the truth about this boy. Briefly I contemplated telling people, one by one, setting the record straight. But this was impractical. I could only stand aside as the coffin was carried from the church to the waiting hearse. But I remember being haunted, later, by the strength of my reaction to Kilroy's parting words.

It turned out, you see, that even before the funeral, Pat Kilroy knew what had happened outside Harry's on the last night of that terminal summer.

Pat Kilroy knew who had killed Conor Harris. He knew as he stared at the crowd from the vantage of the pulpit. He could have pointed, from his wooden roost, at the boys as they sweated in the crowd.

Outside the church Brendan Harris went to stand by himself with his head heavily lowered. I saw Peter Culhane walk over and shake his hand. They nodded together for a moment. Then Eileen Harris called her husband back.

The hearse pulled slowly away through the crowd. The sun was bright overhead and the leaves of the beech trees shook in a tiny breeze. Suntanned boys, back early from their holidays in Portugal and Marbella and Majorca, shook their heads and comforted their beach-brown girlfriends.

The coffin had been carried from the church by six former Brookfield students, Conor's former teammates.

One of them was Richard Culhane.

He had volunteered to do it.

24

Both Richard Culhane and Barry Fox were offered rugby scholarships by University College, Dublin, even before their Leaving Cert. results had come through. Their college places were guaranteed, in other words. All they had to do was get enough points in their final exams – something no Brookfield boy had ever failed to achieve. Conor Harris was also offered a rugby scholarship. Every year UCD offers to pay fees for half a dozen private-school pupils, usually boys who have performed outstandingly on their school's Senior Cup team. In exchange, the boys play for the UCD team. The UCD team hovers near the top of the Dublin league. It tends to serve as a recruitment resource for the national squad.

Richard Culhane turned his scholarship down.

'Other people need the money more than me, you know?' he said. 'I'll still play for the team, like. But I don't need the scholarship.'

Peter Culhane was full of pride at his son's decision. 'Ah, he's a generous lad,' Peter said. 'We raised him right.'

Conor Harris and Barry Fox both accepted their scholarships. They both, as it turned out, performed excellently in their exams. But they were Brookfield boys. Exam success was expected of them.

Sports scholarship boys at UCD were encouraged to study a subject that seemed relevant to their sporting careers – Physiotherapy, Sports Management, Athletic Performance. But the Brookfield boys stuck to Business.

UCD occupies an enormous campus on the south side of the

city, between Donnybrook and Clonskeagh. Most of the campus was built in the early seventies, and the architecture is uniformly dull and angular. The Quinn School, where the Brookfield boys studied, is an exception. It was built in the opening years of the twenty-first century, and features a laptop area, a contemplation room, a café, and an atrium. It is fitted with wireless Internet access. All Quinn School students are expected to buy their own laptop, and to bring it to class.

Laura Haines was enrolled as a nursing student at UCD. Nobody expected her to pursue nursing as a career. She was taking the long route into medical school, because her exam results, contrary to expectations, had been relatively poor.

Training for the UCD rugby squad was a gruelling experience, but the boys were used to it. They had trained after school every day for three years, doing squats and sit-ups on the old school pitch while Pat Kilroy yelled at them and blew his whistle.

Still, Richard Culhane was more dedicated than most, even at college, even when his social life enjoyed that comfortable expansion that awaits any private-school boy who takes his class with him when he enters university. He trained on the floodlit fields on week nights when there were no team sessions scheduled. He did twenty laps of the college athletic track in the rain. I would see him as I walked to the bus stop. He was always completely absorbed, as if he recognized no other world, as if the answer to all his questions could be found at the end of the track that he was diligently running.

25

One summer, when Conor was two years old, Brendan Harris built a boundary wall between their back garden and the garden next door. He did the job himself because he resented paying for builders.

Conor dug at the deepening trench with a plastic shovel and shouted, 'Helping Daddy with the soundation! Daddy digging the soundation!' He watched as his father worked in noncommittal silence, pausing to drink a glass of water Eileen had brought from the kitchen. Brendan seemed to give off a strange, primitive power as he stood there with his head thrown back, his Adam's apple working as he swallowed. But in those days Conor accepted Brendan's power and mystery without question. It was so easy to love your father when you were small. Perhaps when you were very young, that was how your parents appeared: as though they had been constructed with your love in mind.

One day, I'm gonna get that bastard.

Bang.

This can't be happening. This can't be happening.

Bang.

We fucking showed that little cunt.

Bang.

26

Conor Harris and Laura Haines formalized their relationship at a subdued Friday night party in Fergal Morrison's house in Milltown, less than a week after they had fallen into step beside one another in Donnybrook on Senior Cup final day. They were sitting in a corner of the huge conservatory where Fergal's father kept the snooker table. Fergal was trying to teach his then-girlfriend, Caoimhe Murphy, how to play snooker, and some people were gathered around the small bar by the kitchen door. Conor and Laura sat in a broad wicker chair in the corner and kissed and talked.

'So,' Conor said when the conversation had reached the appropriate point. 'Are you my girlfriend now, or what?'

They listened to the soft clicks and pocks from the snooker table.

Laura giggled. 'I suppose I am.'

That was how it was decided.

I think, by this stage, Conor Harris had realized that he was obsessed with Laura Haines. In particular, he was obsessed with her body. Later that night, in the spare room of Fergal Morrison's house, they saw each other naked for the first time. They didn't have sex, though, not straight away. Laura said she thought a month would be the wisest length of time to wait before they fucked. When the Brookfield boys asked if he had managed to stick it in Laura Haines yet, Conor would smile and say nothing.

People were envious of Conor Harris and Laura Haines, but nobody felt comfortable describing them as a golden couple. While their relationship lasted, Conor seemed too intense and Laura seemed too withdrawn. They weren't quite the perfect match that, later, people would praise Laura and Richard Culhane for being.

You saw Conor and Laura together, and you noticed the strained quality of the attention they gave each other. Conor was always leaning in to catch whatever Laura said. People thought he was doing it to mask what she said from everyone else. People thought that Conor wanted Laura all to himself, that he wanted to be the sole recipient of her spoken feelings.

For a while they were the sort of couple who spend every night out kissing in a corner.

But it wasn't in either of them to be so private, so absorbed. They drifted back into the stream of sociability in less than a month. By Christmas 2003 they had stopped giving off that aura of a prior attachment that stops people chatting you up in nightclubs.

By now they were sleeping together on a regular basis. Laura's house was often empty during the daytime. And then there were parties and weekends away. Laura was on the pill but they used condoms all the time. Nevertheless, in February of 2004, they had a pregnancy scare.

Laura's period was three weeks late. She told Conor not to worry about it.

'How can I *not* worry about it?' Conor said.

'It's fine,' Laura said. 'These things happen. I'll get my period and it'll be fine.'

'What if it isn't?' Conor insisted.

They were having lunch in the café of the Quinn School. Laura was wearing pink tracksuit bottoms and a white Ralph Lauren top with the collar turned up. All the time they were arguing, Conor found himself looking at Laura's tits in the white top.

'*Why* are you so *worried*?' Laura hissed.

'I'm just a bit fucking young to be a father, you know what I mean, babes? I'm not keen on having my life ruined, like.'

'It wouldn't be *your* life,' Laura said. 'Just stop *worrying*.'

'What would you do? If you were having it, like?'

'I'm *not* "having it", Conor.'

'But what would you do if you were?'

'You are freaking me out, Conor Harris. Just stop it.'

'You wouldn't, like, get the old boat to England?'

The muscles of Laura's face were tense. She put her coffee cup back on its saucer and she put the saucer on her tray. She stood up and walked away from the table.

'Fuck's *sake*,' Conor said. He looked around to see if anyone he knew had witnessed Laura's exit.

Richard Culhane was sitting by the window.

Conor went after Laura.

Until the end of the week – when Laura got her period – things were bad between them. Conor said he saw babies everywhere. When they went to the cinema in Dundrum, the movie was preceded by an advertisement for a crisis-pregnancy agency. They had been holding hands, but when they saw the ad they separated and sat subtly apart. When Laura told him her period had arrived, Conor crushed his face against hers in spontaneous relief. From then on, when they had sex, they were extra careful.

One day they went to the Dundrum Town Centre for lunch. Laura said she needed to buy some clothes. Conor tagged along as she drifted through the shops.

In BT2 Laura found a hoodie she liked. It was black and spangled with silver stars.

Conor said, 'I'll buy it for you.'

'No,' Laura said. 'You're like, broke.'

The hoodie cost two hundred and fifty euro.

Conor said, 'Do you want it?'

'It's okay,' Laura said. She tried it on. 'It has this pouch thing,' she complained. 'It makes me look pregnant.'

'God forbid,' Conor said.

'What's that supposed to mean?'

'Nothing.'

'It clearly means something, Conor.'

'I mean, God forbid anything should make you look pregnant. Then you might accidentally look like a normal person.'

They had been fighting about Laura's weight. Conor never got over her mysterious intractability where this issue was concerned. He was bored by her endless shopping and by the way she vigilantly maintained her own appearance.

'Fine,' Laura said. 'Just for that, I won't fucking buy it.'

'But you look good in it. It suits you.'

But Laura refused to buy the hoodie.

I don't want to give the impression that they spent all their time fighting. Or that they didn't have fun together. They did the usual relationship things. They went shopping in the Powerscourt Townhouse Centre. They went to rugby matches together. They sat in Stephen's Green on sunny days. They went walking on the strand at Sandymount. They had dinner in Indian restaurants. They went to the movies.

This went on until April 2004, when for no apparent reason Laura met Conor for coffee in the Arts Café in UCD and told him she couldn't see him anymore.

Just over a month later she was going out with Richard Culhane.

Everybody said they were surprised it took so long.

Why did Laura break up with Conor?

I keep asking the same question here, but I no longer expect an answer. The question I keep asking takes various forms, but it always begins with the same word. That word is *Why*?

Why?

Why?

Why?

Why did Laura break up with Conor? He suspected it had something to do with him asking her whether she'd get an abortion if she turned out to be pregnant. He suspected it had something to do with his obsessiveness, with the fact that, in Laura's words, 'He kept staring at my tits all the time.'

I don't think either of these theories is entirely satisfactory.

I think it had something to do with the fact that Laura was, and always had been, in love with Richard Culhane.

So why did Laura go out with Conor in the first place? Richard was single on Senior Cup final day in 2003. There were no reasons Laura couldn't go out with him. So why did she choose Conor instead?

Why?

Conor took the break-up very badly. He went straight to the college bar and began a bender that lasted for two whole days. During that first afternoon he smoked two packs of cigarettes and began to feel ill. After seven or eight hours of ordering pints and shots and chasers – seven or eight hours during which he felt his chest begin to constrict and his breathing become painful – he went looking for Laura in the library, where he was asked to leave because he was making too much noise. He rang up Fergal Morrison and said, 'Laura ended it, man. I need a shoulder.'

Fergal met up with Conor and they went to Russell's in Rane-lagh. Later Fergal would testify that Conor had tried to start a fight on the street outside with a Trinity student who asked Conor for a light for his cigarette. No one else who was there – Dave Whelehan, Caoimhe Murphy, some Brookfield boys – remembers this. Fergal may or may not have made it up to help Richard Culhane's defence. I think I prefer to imagine that it did happen. It was the sort of thing Conor would have done on the night his girlfriend dumped him.

Laura told me Conor tried to call her seven or eight times that night. She refused to answer her phone. 'I thought he should have had, like, more self-respect,' she said. She said she felt sorry for him but there was nothing she could do. 'He just had to deal, like anyone else.'

Conor's aggression was one of the things Laura said she liked least about him. 'But I suppose you kind of have to accept it, if you're going out with a rugby player,' she would say, with the faintest trace of pride.

In January of 2004 Conor had stepped in to defend Laura's honour when she was hassled by a Blackrock boy in a nightclub in Rathmines. Nobody threw any punches but Laura said the atmosphere was 'pretty heavy'. She was smiling as she said it, but I don't think she was aware of this smile, or of the way she played with her hair as she told the story.

I think the truth is that violence turned Laura on. I think she liked the sense of power and threat that people like Conor Harris and Richard Culhane were capable of giving off. She liked men who made her feel physically small. She liked men who were on her side.

It's probable – though I have no evidence to prove it – that Laura cheated on Conor at least once. If you had put this theory to any of Laura's friends at the time, they wouldn't have been surprised. They wouldn't even have asked who you thought Laura was being unfaithful with.

That part was obvious.

When Conor's bender was over he went home to the house in Donnybrook. He arrived at dinner time, just as Eileen was serving chilli con carne with rice, but he said he wasn't hungry and went upstairs to his room. He lay face down on his bed and did something he would only ever tell one other person about: he cried himself to sleep.

I've never doubted that Conor Harris was in love with Laura Haines, just as I've never doubted that Richard Culhane was in love with her, too; just as I've never doubted that Laura loved only Richard, and that she loves him still, even now that he has left for Inishfall and she is here, with the rest of us, alone, bereft.

27

The third thing that made the boys different from any other group of rich young men was that they were the sons of the men who ran the country.

Brookfield boys went on to become senior civil servants, investment bankers, lawyers, doctors, ministers, judges, accountants, property developers, entrepreneurs. When they had sons, they sent them to Brookfield.

Blaise Pascal (1623–1662) argued that hereditary monarchy was the best system of rule because it obviated the need for conflict. If you say, 'Let the wisest man rule!' you get a bloody civil war over who's the wisest. If you say, 'Let the king's son rule!' everyone points to the king's son and says, 'He is our king!'

Semper et Ubique Fidelis.

28

I've never been to Inishfall but Conor Harris had. He went there the summer he turned eleven years old.

Richard Culhane and Conor Harris were in the same primary-school class. This was played up during media coverage of the case but no journalist, so far as I can tell, worked out what it meant.

What it meant was that Richard Culhane and the boy he killed were childhood friends.

Their friendship reached its peak when they were both in fifth class at the Mary Immaculate Primary School for Boys. Mary Immaculate occupies private grounds near Stillorgan. It was built in the early eighties and opened by the then-president of the Republic, Paddy Hilary. It is still the most expensive fee-paying primary school in Dublin, and naturally both the Harrises and the Culhanes were keen to send their children there. A few days after Peter Culhane signed his unborn son up for Brookfield, he signed him up for Mary Immaculate. The Harrises signed Conor up when he was five months old.

The more I think about the lives that Richard and Conor led, the more it seems to me that their fates were beyond their own control. This never seems to have occurred to either of them. They accepted their lives without a murmur: the private schools, the capable and energetic friends, the beautiful houses.

When you're a child, school feels less like an experience and more like a destiny. For Conor and Richard (and for everyone else in this story), I think this feeling went far beyond school. I think it extended to their entire adult lives – or would have so extended, given another outcome.

If Conor had lived, for example.

So Richard and Conor arrived in Mary Immaculate in the same year. They had the same teachers and they did the same homework. They didn't become friends until towards the end of the summer after fourth class. They sat beside each other one afternoon and made each other laugh.

They had both just that month become altar boys at their local church. This meant that their friendship retained its impetus when the school year ended. They played soccer together and rode their bicycles and they climbed trees and did all the other things that boys do on summer holidays. Conor became a fixture at the Culhanes' house in Sandycove. Richard visited the Harrises' house less often. Friendships in school often develop an imbalance of hospitality. The boys thought nothing of it, though Eileen Harris often fretted about how little the Harrises did for Richard.

Conor and Richard became best friends, in the offhand way peculiar to young boys. In other words, they didn't think or talk about each other except when they were spending time in each other's company.

'What about calling Richard?' Brendan Harris would suggest as Conor moped about the house on a Sunday afternoon.

'Oh yeah,' Conor would say, as if this thought had never struck him.

When the summer holidays rolled around Richard told Conor he would be going to Inishfall with his parents for six weeks. Eventually – the usual phone calls having been made, the usual bargaining conducted with Brendan and Eileen Harris – it was agreed that Conor could spend two weeks of his summer holiday in the big white house that belonged to Richard's grandmother.

The Culhanes went down in early June. A week later Brendan Harris drove Conor to the train station.

'Are you sure you'll be alright?' he asked.

'Dad, I'll be *fine*,' Conor said.

'You know you can ask the guard for help if you need it.'

'I'm looking forward to it,' Conor said. 'I don't get the chance to be alone much.'

This was something Conor had heard his mother say a week ago as she prepared for a train journey north to visit her sister.

Peter and Richard Culhane picked Conor up from the station in Tralee and drove Conor out to Inishfall.

The island is a half-kilometre from the country's western edge. A ferry runs irregularly, even though the village of Inishfall proper is connected to the mainland by a recently built concrete road bridge. During seasonal tides it's possible to walk to the island from the mainland. On either side of the bridge, as Peter Culhane drove the boys across it, there stretched a scuffed, tan mile of mirrory sand.

'Spring tide,' Richard said knowledgeably. 'We'll be able to find crabs in the rock pools near the house.'

'What's a spring tide?' Conor asked.

'We did them in geography,' Richard said. 'Like, four times a year the tide goes out really, really far?'

'Oh yeah,' Conor said.

The village itself was tiny: as they drove through it on the way to the house Conor saw a cluster of decrepit cottages ascending a steep street above a small fishing pier. At the top of this mild incline stood a country church with a pointed spire. A soft grey light filled the space between the seafront houses and the rock of the dismal harbour. Triangles of bunting – the remains of some summer festival – still clung damply to the peeling walls. In a fenced-off field a Friesian heifer browsed, flattered by its entourage of flies.

On the lawn of the big white house Katherine Culhane was waiting. Conor got out of the car and followed Richard across the wiry, seashell-pitted grass. The whole place smelled like some nautical catastrophe – like the rusted wreck of a brine-eaten trawler. Conor stepped over the scabbed, thorny crescent of a crab's broken shell and shook hands with Katherine Culhane, who held a glass of wine, although it was only – Conor thought, with a sense of how gleefully his mother would disapprove – four in the afternoon.

They had dinner in the conservatory, with its view of the darkening sea. Once inside the house Conor was cosily reminded of home:

here he found the same recessed lights and costly furniture that seemed to have been issued to every Dublin house he had ever visited.

After dinner Richard said he was tired and wanted to go to bed early. Conor, suddenly lost and homesick, said he would do the same. Peter said he thought this was a good idea.

Conor brushed his teeth in water that tasted salty, and he had an unpleasant, nonsensical image of Peter Culhane laying pipes on the beach, siphoning off seawater to save money on the family's utility bills. In the near-darkness he lay in the unfamiliar bedroom listening for familiar sounds. But there was only the rasping sound of Peter Culhane, coughing and snuffling in the room next door.

Richard had only pretended that he was tired. While Conor lay awake in the room beneath him, Richard sat on his bed in the attic room playing a computer game and thinking.

Although he enjoyed the role of host – on that first afternoon he gave Conor a rapid tour of the island's secret spots – Richard mildly resented Conor's visit. He had developed the conviction that their friendship was a schoolbound affair, and that to drag it so peremptorily into the sacred space of the summer holidays was to subject it to pressures it had never been designed to withstand. He was also conscious, for the first time, of the fact that Conor's family *didn't* own a second house to which they could retreat every summer. He noticed that Conor was unfamiliar with things like spring tides and sailboats. In fact, Richard had begun to see himself as Conor's economic and intellectual superior, and he was aware that his own capacity for pity wouldn't be enough to see him through the two weeks they were supposed to spend together.

The next morning both of the boys felt measurably better. After breakfast they climbed down the sandy dunes to the beach and went hunting in the shallow pools near the shoreline. By lunchtime they each carried a seething bucket of captured crabs. Conor's interest in the creatures was almost scientific. He watched them scrabble and scrape at the sides of the bucket, climbing over one another to get to the top.

Katherine made them leave the buckets outside while they had lunch. When they had finished eating Richard proposed that they reintroduce the crabs to their natural habitat. By now the tide had come in, so they stood on a small bluff overlooking the water and competed to see who could throw a crab the farthest. Finally they began hurling the crabs against the rocks that protruded from the sandy soil near the house, judging the results in terms of splatter and limb-loss.

When they got bored of this they began a circuit of the island. They paused at a walled orchard to steal some apples, which they threw at cattle until a man on a bicycle shouted at them to stop.

'I should show you the secret beach,' Richard said.

The secret beach was a small windswept cove on the western side of the island. When the boys reached it, crossing as they went the damp, compacted sand of the sheltered dunes, they found that some people were already there: a couple with their two small children.

'It's no good if there's someone here,' Richard complained.

But Conor was happy they had run across some other people. All afternoon they had been alone, and to Conor the island was beginning to seem desolate, abandoned.

By now the boys' mood was feverish, hysterical. They had been tackling each other as they ran to the secret beach, giggling uncontrollably and shouting obscenities into the breeze that was gusting in off the coast. Now Richard stood on the bluff that overlooked the cove and frowned as he caught his breath.

Conor saw that finding strangers at the cove had altered Richard's mood. A part of him was aware of the fragility of Richard's comfort. He had sensed a faint hostility in some of the things Richard had said as they traversed the island ('How could you *never* have caught a crab before? That's, like, so basic'). He was never sure, afterward, why he did what he did next.

What he did next was to scramble up on to the bluff beside Richard and wave madly at the people on the beach.

'Hey!' he shouted, giggling. 'Hey, get the fuck off our beach!'

The people on the beach turned to look at the two boys. Conor slapped Richard on the shoulder and started to run. He was still laughing as he ran along the edge of the bluff. He was still laughing as he looked back and saw Richard lunge after him, jumping across a gap in the bluff and landing heavily and awkwardly on the hillock on the other side. He was still laughing when he saw Richard tumble and fall.

Conor stopped running. Such was his exhilaration, he found himself jumping on the spot as he looked back at the spot where he had seen Richard drop from view.

He ran back to the edge of the gap and looked down. Seven or eight feet below Richard law sprawled on a rocky outcrop. It was immediately obvious that he had landed on his backside.

Already the people at the cove were climbing over the low rocks and coming towards them.

Conor, who had never entirely stopped laughing, stood on the bluff and pointed down at Richard, who stared up at him, his eyes huge with fury and embarrassment. Now Conor's laughter increased in volume and complexity. He pointed down at his friend, who sat in what was surely the most ridiculous of positions: rubbing his bruised backside and glaring incredulously upwards.

The people from the cove arrived and hurried over to Richard, who by this time had started to cry.

Conor continued to laugh, in amusement and delight. He wasn't able to stop. He knew he had gained an advantage over Richard. All the authority in their unbalanced friendship seemed suddenly to have accrued to him.

It soon became evident that Richard was acting like someone who had been quite badly hurt.

'High jinks, lads,' said the father of the children they had seen playing on the secret beach, shaking his head parentally.

He helped Richard to his feet. Richard's hands and forearms had been scratched by briars and wiry grass as he fell. He had twisted his ankle, though not so badly that he was unable to walk.

When Conor had stopped laughing – when the seeming seriousness of the situation had imposed itself on him – he climbed down and told the people from the cove that he would help Richard walk back to the big white house. And so he did: the two boys walked home in silence, Richard with the pursed, frowning face of someone deeply insulted, Conor with the thickening heart of someone who knows he has made a mistake.

When they got to the house Katherine Culhane, roused from her afternoon nap, made a show of tending to Richard. She put iodine on the cuts on his hands and made him iced tea while he lay on the couch in the conservatory.

Silently the boys had agreed to pretend that Richard had fallen by accident, that no one had been there to see it, and that Conor had acted with prompt and becoming solicitude when he found his friend was injured.

For two days Richard refused to speak to Conor. Because neither of them was willing to let Peter and Katherine know that they had fallen out, they sat in the same rooms and pretended to play together. Richard laboured over video games and waited for his ankle to heal. Conor read comics and adventure stories and felt miserable.

On the morning of the third day Richard invited Conor to play football on the beach.

As far as I'm aware, neither of them ever mentioned Richard's fall in each other's company again. Certainly they never mentioned Conor's laughter.

When school resumed in September, Conor and Richard were no longer friends.

Richard never told anyone about what had happened on Inishfall. Conor, I think, told Laura. And he told one other person, who had no way of checking if it was true.

I adduce it now as one more reason, one more unsettled score. Is it enough? Did Richard Culhane kill Conor Harris outside Harry's Niteclub in Blackrock on 31 August 2004, because when they were eleven years old Richard fell on his backside and Conor laughed? Is this enough of a reason? Is this why Conor had to die?

('Harry's Niteclub'. How inured I've become to that tritely pervasive misspelling. When I think about it now it seems to have become emblematic of the Harris case in all its garish mundanity: a glaring error in gleamingly permanent neon.)

No. What happened on Inishfall isn't enough of a reason for Conor's death. Perhaps no reason is sufficient in itself. Perhaps they don't even add up to a satisfactory whole. Perhaps – though I find this notion hard to take – there simply is no reason, none at all, not even the usual, rudimentary suspects like *It was an accident,* or *It was meant to happen,* or *It was just his time, man. It was just his time.*

Bang.

Bang.

BANG.

Richard's fall. I wonder about this. He had fallen only seven or eight feet and had landed, rocks notwithstanding, mostly on soft sand. The cuts and scrapes on his hands and arms looked bad, but they healed in a couple of days. What was wounded, of course, was his dignity, that aspect of his character that Richard, even as a child, treated with the most respect, that quality that was sometimes mistaken (by the media, for example) for pomposity. Richard had elected himself Conor's superior, in knowledge, in money, in maturity. And here was Conor, laughing at his pain. To Richard, this was not a forgivable offense.

But I don't know if he brooded on it for longer than the two days it took him to make his peace with Conor. I don't even know if Richard, in later life, *remembered* his fall from the bluff, or Conor's reaction to it. There is no way of knowing, because he never brought it up.

Nonetheless, it's an image that keeps coming back to me, Richard Culhane falling from the edge of a sandy bluff above a windswept beach. Again and again I see it, Richard falling, Richard vanishing from sight, Richard dropping though a gap in the ground and suddenly, painfully, disappearing, as if he had been pulled back into the earth by something that badly wanted him there – gravity, perhaps, or fate.

29

When Laura hadn't eaten, her breath would smell like sour milk, and Conor would try to avoid her kisses. She had explained about her problems with food, which to Conor's family was like having problems with furniture or air. You don't question the elements, his mother would say from behind the clattering turret of her sewing machine. And Conor agreed with her, although he was in love, and positive that Laura's problems didn't matter.

There was something weary about his mother's wisdom, Conor thought, as though it had come to her too late. He listened to her, fascinated, wary of showing how much her sayings meant to him. Boys were supposed to shock their mothers, to turn their warmth and kindness upside down, but Conor was always made tender by his mother's vulnerability. He was childishly interested in what she had to say.

Since retiring from the hands-on side of the family's restaurant business, Eileen Harris worked desultorily from home, selling patchwork quilts of her own design and, occasionally, cushions and throws that wound up in the unused living rooms of her wealthy friends and neighbours. Their neighbourhood in Donnybrook was like that: full of people who could afford to have a room they never used. Laura came from such a house, which she once described to Conor as 'an ordinary six-bedroom family house', and which always astonished him with its pristine permanence whenever he entered it. Every surface in that house would gleam and glitter. The rooms contained a silken hush, as though they expected you to be as neat and calm as they were. The kitchen was full of marble and stainless steel, and appeared never to have been used for anything so mundane as the preparation of food.

Certainly Laura would never have used it for such a task. She hardly touched food if she could help it. She greeted the suggestion of lunch with wan indifference. Conor never saw it as a problem. After his death I forgot about Laura's eating disorder, and when I remembered it, sitting down to write this account, it had somehow become lapidary, inevitable, a part of the past. Perhaps more strangely, it had become something to do with Conor. It had become just one more fact about the dead.

30

As Conor got older, Brendan Harris learned to be awkward with his son. This was what men of their class and generation did: they found each others' private lives embarrassing. Peter Culhane had always been blustery and vague with Richard. It came naturally to him. He had learned from his father. But Brendan Harris had to work it out for himself.

Brendan took his cue from his son. Shortly after Conor arrived at Brookfield he began to call his father 'Dave'. To his school friends, habitually, Conor referred to his parents as 'the old pair'. Both of these things were ways of denying that you had parents at all.

On a Saturday afternoon in May Brendan found Conor sitting on an old iron bench in the back garden of the Harrises' house in Donnybrook. This was a week after Conor and Laura had broken up. Little fragments of browning mayflower dropped from the hawthorn tree above the bench. Brendan walked slowly down the garden with his hands in the pockets of his slacks.

Conor had spent the last two days lying in his room, listening to Alice in Chains records that he had borrowed from his brother. Now here he was, sitting in the sun, wearing wraparound Ray-Bans and drinking a fizzy drink.

'Alright, Con?' Brendan said.

'Yeah,' Conor said.

'Feeling a bit better?'

'Yeah.'

Eileen Harris had hung a bronze windchime from a branch of the hawthorn tree. It shook and shivered in the cooling breeze.

'How do you think the exams went?' Brendan asked.

'Fine,' Conor said.

There was a silence.

'I know it's hard,' Brendan said.

'What?'

'Dealing with … you know, matters of the heart.'

'Is it?'

'Yeah,' Brendan said. He frowned at an unweeded flowerbed. 'It is. We've all been through it, you know.'

'No,' Conor said. 'No we haven't.'

'I went through it,' Brendan said.

'Good for you,' Conor said.

Brendan was offended by this. He was offended by Conor's refusal to acknowledge that his experience was not unique. To Brendan Harris, heartbreak was soothingly universal. The way you got through it was to share your pain with someone else.

But I think Conor was right, in one way at least. He could never have conveyed to Brendan what it meant to lose Laura Haines.

Again Brendan frowned at the unweeded flowerbed. Then he turned and went inside.

Conor sat on the bench. After a few minutes he heard the hollow pocking sound of Brendan practising putts in the garage, sending the pitted balls with their core of childhood mystery (was it poison? glue? the hardest substance known to man?) rattling into a tin can saved from the recycling bin.

Only once did I ever hear Conor talk about his father. His tone was baffled, almost hurt. 'Sometimes you look at your old man,' he said, 'and you wonder, what the fuck do you think of me, really? I mean, who *are* you, anyway?'

Richard Culhane would not have sympathized with this. He viewed his father with a mixture of pious scorn and exasperated love. Even when Richard was in his late teens – shaving twice a day, sleeping at his girlfriend's house, drinking, driving – Peter would still tousle his son's hair at the breakfast table.

'He hasn't noticed I'm a grown-up yet,' Richard said.

You can see a larger truth in this. Our parents all suffered from the same reluctance to let us go. They loved and understood us when we were children, but when we became adults they found us too complicated, too alien, too wilfully self-destructive. Suddenly we made no sense. The only skills our parents could summon were skills that applied to us as kids. We came to resent them for this, for their inability to relinquish a tone of faintly condescending intimacy, and for the abrupt way in which they stood revealed to us as amateurs, sad approximations of our professional selves in our newfound confidence and nous.

And yet we took their prosperity for granted. We lived in houses they had bought and went on holidays that they had paid for. We saw our parents, as all children eventually do, as separate from the things that they had done for us. So it was never a question of gratitude. That wasn't the way it worked.

Sometimes I would look around my parents' house and wonder by what miracle, what unimaginable system of bargains and balances, it had come into being. In my late teens I began to realize that our house had not occurred by parthenogenesis, that it had not sprung into existence an instant before my birth, but that my parents had bought it and furnished it and made it what it was, one task at a time, all before I had even been thought of. I couldn't imagine ever doing such a thing myself.

In the aftermath of Conor's death people would often say of Richard Culhane or Barry Fox or Stephen O'Brien (or even of Conor himself), 'He had it easy.' This isn't true, of course. Life is easy for no one. But it is true that these boys were born into a life that had been sanded down, smoothed over. It was a polished life, one with no rough edges – or none, at least, beyond the universal pains and worries. But this polishing, this sanding down, had already been finished by the time the boys arrived. They had nothing to add to its completion. All they had to do was keep it going.

I often wonder what effect this had on them – on their generation. They may never have thought about it, of course. Or it might have occurred to them only later, after the fact, after their unquestioned claim on this prepared existence had, agonizingly, vanished.

As he practised his putts in the garage Brendan Harris remembered the easy intimacy he had had with his son when Conor was a child.

Conor's birth had been difficult. Eileen Harris laboured for fourteen hours before her second son showed his face. He looked red and embittered, as though he had seen something in the womb that had disgusted him beyond belief. He grew up to be a strong man – physically strong, I mean; he had the strong man's fondness for, and impatience with, delicate things – but he never lost the aftershock of that first vinegary frown, that air of having known corruption early and seen it clearly for what it was.

When Conor died Brendan forgot about this first, sour expression on his son's pink face. We forget things like this about the dead because there is nothing to remind us of them.

31

Claire Lawrence had been a cutter, but Laura Haines was different. She was in control. She was together. She wasn't a mess. Of course Richard had known Laura for years. But the force of this truth – that she was self-sufficient, even imperious, that most of the time she didn't even seem to need him – only struck him properly when she had become, officially, his girlfriend.

Richard Culhane and Laura Haines were sitting on the ground beneath a copper beech in the grounds of Brookfield when they first kissed. It was a Sunday afternoon in the early May of 2004. They had walked along the pier at Dun Laoghaire and then they had caught the DART to Blackrock and bought cheese and wine in Marks & Spencer. As they crossed the road at the gate of Brookfield Richard took Laura's hand. They sat beneath the copper beech and gossiped about Laura's friends. They ignored the cheese but drank the wine from paper cups. After an interval of silence (the breeze, the sunlight, the sound of Sunday traffic), Richard leaned over and kissed Laura.

'It's about *time*,' Laura said happily.

They sat under the tree until it got cold and they had to go home.

Despite Richard's beauty and his facility in conversation (he could talk knowledgeably about any number of surprising subjects, from house prices to wine to French politics), he hadn't gone out with very many girls. In fact, he would probably have described himself, a little wistfully, as a man still in search of his one true love. This was a part of his charm: people were reassured by the fact that even Richard, with his prodigal gifts as a student, a son, a friend, a lover, still pined for the one soul that would successfully complement his own.

Richard admired his own loneliness. This was something you could sense in him when you saw him practising on a field alone in the rain. I know a part of him feared that he would be compromised by love. But Laura seemed to override this fear.

When did they first meet? I haven't been able to find this out. Richard and Laura seem always to have known one another. They seemed always to show up on the same nights out, to arrive at the same parties, to know the same people and to keep track of the same gossip. In their peculiar way, they were always faithful to one another, though they ignored one another, though they went out with various other people. People found the idea of them seductive. And they agreed with this, I think; they were aware of their own power, their own rosy, unaffected authority. Richard and Laura were, unquestionably, at the centre of things. They gave a veneer of authenticity to any event they attended. Even before they were together, their world – that small south Dublin world of private schools and parties and clubs – arranged itself centrifugally around Richard and Laura. Their relationship had long seemed inevitable, foretold, a fait accompli.

I saw them dance together once, at a party in Dave Whelehan's house. It was the end of the night and a few last couples were dancing to slow music in the kitchen. Laura danced with her head on Richard's chest. Richard kissed the top of Laura's head as they shuffled across the terracotta flagstones. They both seemed sad, though they hadn't fought. I watched them and felt sad, too. The image stayed with me. Even then, the moment seemed to mean something.

I don't think Laura ever danced that way with Conor Harris.

32

'Isn't that one of your friends, Richard?' Katherine Culhane said. She looked around her kitchen, unfairly calm in the morning light. She looked at her son. 'Isn't that awful?'

Perhaps oddly, perhaps not, I think the real moment of change in this story comes not with Conor's death but with the boys' discovery the next morning that they had killed him. This was the moment when the boys became murderers – to themselves, at least, if not in legal terms, if not in the minds of their parents and friends.

This was the moment when they no longer knew who or what they would become.

Picture them in their kitchens, with their orange juice or coffee or tea. Their mothers have turned the radio on, as a matter of course, to listen to the news as they make breakfast for their kids.

It's the top story on *Morning Ireland*. A young man dies after being beaten to death outside a nightclub in Blackrock. The young man has been identified as Conor Harris of Donnybrook, County Dublin. Gardaí are investigating reports that Conor became involved in a fracas moments before he was attacked.

'Isn't that one of your friends, Richard?'

But Richard says nothing, because there is nothing he can say.

33

What did Richard Culhane do when he heard that Conor Harris was dead? He went out into the back garden of the house in Sandycove and looked at his father's swimming pool. His hair was still thatched and tepid from the shower. He had barely slept. It was an overcast morning and rain was gently stippling the glossy surface of the pool. Richard looked into the water and put his hands in his pockets and thought, *I'm fucked.*

Christ, we killed him. We fucking killed him.

(*We fucking showed that little cunt.*)

For several minutes Richard felt bottomlessly calm. He watched the canted corner of a flagstone fill with rain. His mind, so far as he could remember afterwards, was completely blank. He studied the patterns made by the sheeted drizzle on the surface of the pool. He giggled a little, he said. *Hysterical laughter,* is how some people diagnosed this giggle later on. *A nervous reaction.*

Some people weren't so kind.

'And what were you thinking, Mr Culhane?' the prosecution would ask about the moment Richard went out to look at the pool.

Richard blinked. 'Nothing.'

'Nothing at all.'

'I can't remember,' Richard said, 'but I don't think I was thinking anything at all.'

'But you *giggled.*'

Richard, in the witness box, blushed and lowered his head. He had mentioned the giggling once, during a garda interrogation, and it had made the papers. It had become a feature of the case. But the interrogations had exhausted him. In desperation he had told the truth about that moment, which is that he giggled.

What should he have done, he wondered? What had people expected him to do? Drop to his knees? Burst into tears? Scream at the heavens?

Pray?

When Richard was fourteen the family dog, Snowball, got stuck behind the shed at the end of the garden and tore his paw on a rusty nail. Katherine drove Richard and Snowball to the vet in Dun Laoghaire. When Richard got out of the car he saw that Snowball had bled all over his white O'Neills tracksuit bottoms. The vet disinfected Snowball's paw and wrapped it in bandages. As the vet worked, Snowball squirmed and yelped in distress. And Richard stood to one side and giggled helplessly, even though he knew his dog was in pain, even though he knew he himself was really very upset. He giggled.

Hysterical laughter, people told him. *A nervous reaction.*

Richard wanted to explain this in court but he couldn't find the words.

He stood on the flagstones and looked at the surface of the pool.

Christ, he thought, *we killed him.*

Then he nearly threw up.

Richard said he saw his future, then. He saw the whole thing, the arrests and the garda interrogations and the trials and the years in prison. Richard knew that very soon he would be visiting important buildings – buildings where only important things go down: churches, law courts, hospitals. You know you're in trouble when your future is full of important buildings.

I'm fucked, he kept repeating to himself, over and over. *I'm fucked I'm fucked I'm fucked I'm fucked I'm fucked.*

He also thought (strangely, and not for the last time): *Time to go, man. Time to go.*

He bent over and rested his palms on his knees. He was hyperventilating. He thought he might throw up into the swimming pool. Bizarrely, he remembered a morning in Ocean City, the morning after a party in the beachside condo the boys had rented, when he had staggered out on to the verandah at 7 am and deposited a speckled pint of milky vomit in the wilted shrubbery beyond the fence.

He stared at the swimming pool.

I'm fucked, he thought.

Well, then, he told himself. You better not fucking say anything to anyone, Richard my boy.

Richard looked back at the kitchen window and saw that Katherine had gone upstairs. The shock of nausea had passed. With convalescent gravity he took out his mobile phone and dialled Barry Fox's number. Barry Fox was an early riser. He would be awake. He would have heard the news.

'Hello?'

'Foxer, it's Richard. Have you heard this shit?'

'What shit?'

Barry's voice was grizzled, geriatric. Richard heard the sound of a mattress as it creaked under shifting weight.

'Fucking Conor Harris is fucking *dead*, man,' Richard said.

'Why? What did he do?'

'No, I mean he's actually fucking *dead*. As in, like, *not alive anymore*. He fucking died in hospital last night.'

'What? How?' There was a silence. 'Oh *fuck*.'

'It's all over fucking *Morning Ireland*. My fucking *mother* just heard it.'

'Oh fuck. Oh shit.'

'Listen, Foxer, did anyone see us last night? Can anyone, like, identify us, or whatever?'

'How the fuck should I know, man? Did you call Steve?'

'No, calm down, alright, I called you first.'

'Well what the fuck are we going to do?'

'Look, come round to my gaff, alright? We'll have a chat, sort this out.'

'Okay, I'll be there in like half an hour.' There was a pause. 'Dude, does Laura know?'

'I don't know,' Richard said. 'I haven't talked to her.'

'Okay.'

Richard dialled Stephen O'Brien's number.

'Richmeister,' Steve said. His voice was raw. 'What's the story?'

Richard told him.

'Fuck me,' Steve said, very quietly.

Twenty minutes later Barry Fox and Stephen O'Brien were sitting in Richard's living room. It was still raining outside.

'Okay,' Richard said. 'How many people saw the fight?'

'Like, two dozen?' Barry said. 'It was in the middle of the fucking *street*, Richard. The guards are like, already on their way, dude.'

'Don't panic,' Richard said. 'On the news it said they didn't have any suspects yet.'

They were all standing, Richard and Barry by the window, Steve with his backside propped against the sofa. Stephen and Barry were wearing their old red-and-white Brookfield jerseys. Richard had given his to Laura Haines. She slept in it, sometimes. She said it smelled like Richard.

'Christ,' Stephen O'Brien said. 'Have you told Laura yet?'

'For fuck's SAKE, Steve, I'm trying to think about one fucking thing at a time here, alright?'

'Alright, man, keep it together, like.'

For maybe a minute nobody spoke. It was quiet enough for Richard to hear the snicker and hiss of Stephen O'Brien's cheap plastic lighter as he lit a cigarette by the open window. Then Barry Fox said, 'What do we do?'

Richard looked at him. He knew what they had to do.

They didn't talk to their parents. They didn't talk to the guards. They didn't talk to a lawyer. They didn't even talk to each other, not really.

Richard drove them to Blackrock. He drove them to Brookfield and they talked to Pat Kilroy.

They had killed a boy the night before and that morning they talked to the man who had coached them when they played Senior Cup rugby.

34

To Richard, growing older had meant discovering more and more of the unknown in himself, as though he had been a mystery all along, and was only coming to realize it now that he was no longer a child. But as he drove to Brookfield on the morning of 1 September he was full of a strange excitement. He found himself no longer inexplicable. Later he would come to believe that this was because that morning he was confronting the first inarguable truth about himself: that he was capable of murder.

Although it was a Sunday, the boys knew Pat Kilroy would be at the school, training either the Senior or the Junior Cup team for an early-season match. As it happened neither of the teams was training that day, but Pat Kilroy was in his office, drawing up class timetables. Father Connelly was there, too, in the school chapel, writing references for past pupils.

Richard drove up to the courtyard of the school. The engine died. Faint ticks impinged on the sudden silence. The boys sat in the car without moving, Richard and Barry in the front, Stephen sitting alone in the back seat. As they drove the rain had stopped but now it started again, falling on the gravel of the courtyard and blurring the windscreen of Richard's car.

'Let's do it,' Richard said.

Afterwards Richard said that all through that Sunday morning and afternoon he had the feeling that he was in a film, that the occasion called for dramatic dialogue, pithy statement. He only said this in private, of course. He only said it to Laura Haines, who said she kind of understood.

The boys went into their old school. They went up the main stairs, forbidden to students, and knocked on the door of Pat Kilroy's office.

On the wall outside hung the framed newspaper article about Richard Culhane's Senior Cup debut.

Pat opened the door and frowned.

'Lads!' he said. 'Great to see you here. What brings you to these parts?'

'Hiya Pat,' Barry said. 'Can we have a word with you?'

Pat showed them into the office and they sat on the chairs in front of his desk. When they had studied at Brookfield they had only ever sat in these chairs when they were in trouble.

Pat Kilroy sat at his desk and looked at the boys.

'What's up?' he asked.

The boys didn't look at each other. They looked at the floor or the desk.

Richard said, 'Did you listen to the radio this morning, sir?'

'No, why?' Pat said. 'Is everything all right, lads?'

They told him Conor Harris was dead.

'*What?*' Pat Kilroy said.

'We didn't know he was dead,' Barry Fox said. 'We didn't know he was dead, sir. We didn't mean to do anything like that. It was just an accident. It was just an accident.'

'Shut up, Barry,' Stephen O'Brien said.

There were tears in Barry Fox's eyes.

'What are you saying?' Pat Kilroy said. 'You're saying that Conor Harris, who went to this school, died last night?'

Pat Kilroy was very good at his job. He had already thought about the phone call to Conor's parents, the words he would speak at the funeral if he was asked, the memorial service in the school chapel. Barry's words about it being an accident hadn't registered with him yet. That took another minute.

Richard said, 'We heard it on the news this morning.'

'And you say there was an accident?' Pat Kilroy said. He looked searchingly at Barry Fox.

'Yeah,' Richard said.

'We saw Conor at a club last night,' Stephen O'Brien said.

'... And what happened to him?' Pat Kilroy said.

'There was a bit of a fight, sir.'

Pat Kilroy turned down the corners of his mouth. 'And were ye three involved in this fight?'

'Yeah,' Stephen said.

Pat Kilroy looked at the three hulking children sitting in front of his desk. 'Ah, lads,' he said.

This was the only time that Pat Kilroy allowed the fear and disappointment he felt to enter his voice. The boys flinched when he said it: *Ah, lads.* They had grown up listening to Pat Kilroy bawl at them on the rugby pitch, telling them to get their act together, stop acting like little girls, for Christ's sake not to be so fucking wussy. But *Ah, lads,* that was the killer: in that tone of quaking apprehension, that tone of unbearable disappointment.

Stephen O'Brien said afterwards that this was the moment he realized he was really in the shit.

Strange to say, up until this point none of the boys had thought about Conor Harris or his family. They had barely thought about themselves. They had been trained not to examine their own feelings too closely. To Richard and Stephen and Barry, those two words of Pat Kilroy – *Ah, lads* – instantly overturned fifteen years of education. They were forced to acknowledge that they had trespassed on the world of the irrevocable: of things that could not be taken back.

Ah, lads.

'Tell me what happened,' Pat Kilroy said.

'He started on us,' Stephen O'Brien said.

Barry said tiredly, 'He started on Richard.'

Richard nodded. 'He used to go out with my girlfriend.'

'Is that what this was about?' Pat Kilroy asked.

There was a moment of silence.

This moment of silence in Pat Kilroy's office in Brookfield could, I think now, have been the moment that obviated everything that followed, all the questions, all the misdirected blame. This moment was Richard's chance to tell the truth, or at least to admit that the truth was more complicated than the question of who was fucking Laura Haines, that it was more complicated than a single incident outside a nightclub at three o'clock in the morning, that it was more complicated than a schoolyard betrayal or a drunken mistake. This could have been the moment when every question about motive was settled, when the boys admitted what has become increasingly clear as time goes by and we all achieve a little distance from Conor's death: that nobody knew *why* Conor had to die, that there was no good reason for it, that it was simply in the nature of the way these people lived.

All we know is that he died. Anything else is a whistle in the dark.

Richard didn't say anything. Then he said, 'Yeah.'

Pat Kilroy looked at the three boys in turn. He was used to dealing with the painful transparency of young men, of course. He had become immune to it. But here was something else. The thought occurred to him: *They might as well be infants screaming in their mothers' arms.*

And another thought: *Their lives are over.*

Richard looked at the man on the other side of the desk. He could see Pat Kilroy strenuously wish that he smoked a pipe or did the crossword, or had some other intricate masculine ritual in which he could bury his discomfort and fright. He sensed that Pat Kilroy was at a loss. He was aware of what this meant. It meant that the usual resources were already failing.

But Kilroy rallied. He stood and went to the office window, his hands behind his back.

'Right,' he said, and cleared his throat. 'Now I know you're probably a bit panicky about this. That's understandable. But you know, of course, that *we will do everything in our power* to make sure that things work out for the best.'

He didn't need to tell the boys who he meant by *we.*

(But if you had asked any of the four men in that room directly, 'Who do you mean by *we*?' they would not have been able to answer.)

Pat Kilroy said, 'You were right to come to me, lads.'

The boys were perceptibly happy to hear this. They stretched minutely. Their shoulders sagged. Pat Kilroy experienced a sudden startling influx of nostalgia: for his own school days, for his two years on the SCT, for the period, now forever lost, before the three boys with their heavy treads had arrived at his office door to ask for help.

And that the boys had asked for help – though the words were never spoken – Pat Kilroy never seriously doubted. In addition, it never occurred to him to wonder why the boys had not gone first of all to their parents with their suffering. To Pat Kilroy it seemed just, even inevitable, that the boys had brought their burden to him first.

Other people have wondered, though – people, it hardly needs to be said, who did not receive a private education, who never attended a Jesuit school, who never played for a Senior Cup team. To understand why the boys went first to Pat Kilroy, you have to understand the centrality and significance in their lives of rugby, that game of snaps and tackles, of maulings and drubbings and three-yard runs. When the boys went out and got drunk, they talked about rugby: about Brian O'Driscoll and Ronan O'Gara and Ireland's chances in the Six Nations. For all three boys, rugby was almost the only thing they had in common with their fathers. Most of the important emotions they experienced on a daily basis had to do with rugby; had to do with victory and sacrifice, profit and pain, all experienced within the confines of the sport – but no less valid or genuine for that. And Pat Kilroy had been the man who took them through it, who knew how to solve their problems, who knew how to resurrect their confidence, who knew how to succour them in their defeat.

'What I want you to do,' Pat Kilroy said, 'is tell me everything that happened, as far as you can remember it.'

So they told him everything that happened, as far as they could remember it. They omitted certain details: the three kicks, for example, and the number of drinks they'd had. They left out *We fucking showed that little cunt.* They left out the sense of charged release they felt when they finally got to punch Conor Harris in the face.

When they had finished Pat Kilroy was sitting at his desk, leaning back in his chair with his eyes closed. During the narrative – Stephen O'Brien had taken charge of a great deal of the telling – Pat Kilroy had nodded, but made no comment. Now he leaned forward and rested his elbows on the creaking leather of his desk.

'This is a terrible thing,' he said. 'That a young man could lose his life over something so small.'

The three boys looked at the floor. It had never occurred to them to see the incident in this light. The first thing they had thought of was their own complicity. Now they realized that a boy they knew had died: a realization simultaneously pathetic and annoying. *Why did he have to fucking* die? Barry Fox remembered thinking at this point.

Pat Kilroy sniffed and shook his head. 'You were right to come to me,' he said again. 'What we need to do is get this down on paper. Just so we have a record of the truth. And,' he shifted irritably, 'so ye can clarify everything to yourselves. How would you feel if I asked Father Connelly up here to help us?'

The boys nodded dumbly.

'Alright. I'll go down and ask him up. Don't panic, now, lads. It's all in hand.'

Pat Kilroy was gone for five minutes. During this time none of the three boys spoke or moved. They were conscious of requiring official approval, official observation, for their smallest action. They were conscious that if good behaviour started now, then whatever happened later on could be mitigated, softened.

Father Connelly embraced the boys when he arrived. Then he listened to what they had to say and agreed with Pat Kilroy that some sort of written statement was in order. It was proposed that each of the three boys write a short account of what had happened, and that they should confer with one another as they wrote to make sure that their versions concurred in every respect. Then Pat Kilroy and Father Connelly would sign the statements and keep them at the school.

The boys recognized in this plan the imprimatur of an authority greater than themselves. They submitted to it gratefully.

It took them half an hour to write the statements. As Richard handed his to Pat Kilroy he said, 'And you'll hang on to this, won't you, sir? In case we need it.'

'I'll hang on to it,' Pat Kilroy said. 'I'll keep it in the safe. It won't fall into the wrong hands and it will always be here if you need it.'

Kilroy and Father Connelly read the statements – none of them longer than a single sheet of foolscap – and signed them. The boys had wanted to write on official school paper – they had wanted to see the Brookfield crest and its motto (*Semper et Ubique Fidelis*) in the upper right-hand corner. Pat Kilroy had been doubtful about this, but he had relented.

'Thank you, sir,' Richard said, when the statements had been witnessed.

During his years on the SCT Richard had always called Mr Kilroy 'Pat'. Now 'sir' seemed to have been dragged out of him by the obsequiousness of guilt – or by his sudden awareness of his youth, his childishness, his lack of sophistication.

Richard, Barry and Stephen watched as Pat Kilroy sealed the statements in an envelope and deposited them in the safe concealed (the boys observed with fleeting wonder) behind a large photo of the Brookfield Senior Cup team from 1978.

Then Father Connelly knelt and led them all in prayer.

'Our father, who art in heaven,' he said. 'Hallowed be thy name. Thy Kingdom come, thy will be done, on earth as it is in heaven. Give us this day our daily bread, and forgive us our trespasses, as we forgive those who trespass against us. And lead us not into temptation, but deliver us from evil. Amen.'

'Amen,' said Stephen O'Brien, Barry Fox and Richard Culhane.

'Amen,' said their old headmaster.

When the boys had left, Pat Kilroy locked the door of his office and sat at his desk for a long time. Then he finished his morning's work – those troublesome timetables – and closed his briefcase. When he got to his car he stopped and looked back at the main building of the school. He turned a slow half-circle in valedictory appraisal. He took in the courtyard, the copper beech, the low outhouses that served as locker rooms.

He had taken the statements with him in his briefcase.

He didn't want to keep them at the school.

35

If those statements still existed, we would all, perhaps, know a great deal more about why Conor died. But Pat Kilroy destroyed them on the day the three boys were arrested. He fed them to the fire in the living room of his house on Mount Merrion Avenue in Blackrock. He has never explained why he thought this necessary.

There are several theories. One: the statements incriminated the boys to a degree that Kilroy found disturbing. Two: the story told by the statements contained one or more aspects that the gardaí already knew to be untrue, and Pat Kilroy destroyed the documents to save the boys from being charged with obstruction of justice. Three: the burden of responsibility entailed by possession of the statements became too much for Pat Kilroy to bear. Four: the statements in themselves were insufficient to exonerate the boys, and Kilroy believed that they would simply contribute to their eventual undoing. Five: Pat Kilroy wanted to avoid causing undue pain to the boys' parents – and to Eileen and Brendan Harris.

There is a sixth theory. It is possible that the statements portrayed the lives and behaviour of Brookfield graduates in a way that Pat Kilroy found unacceptable, and he destroyed them for this reason alone.

An opinion-piece published in a reputable broadsheet had the following to say about Pat Kilroy and the missing statements:

> It's not often you get to catch the old boys' network in a rearguard action, trying desperately to defend three of its own. But that's what these statements essentially were, whatever they may have

contained. This was one public schoolboy buying insurance for three more public schoolboys. Did Pat Kilroy keep those signed confessions in a big brown envelope? He might as well have. Brown envelopes have always been how you got ahead in the Republic. Just don't try it if you grew up in Darndale. That's what we've got in this country: one law for the rich and another for the poor.

This article expressed a sentiment that was shared by many people. Of course, the matter of the secret statements was just one tiny aspect of what people viewed as a larger failure of justice: the cancelled trial that, eventually, allowed Richard to go free. But it was seized on, nonetheless, as one more sign that the country's rulers were not prepared to sacrifice 'three of their own', even for so grave a crime as murder.

I don't question the validity of this argument. But I think Pat Kilroy's motivations, when he helped the boys compose their statements and offered to keep them hidden in the Brookfield safe, derived from a more complex source than the demands of class loyalty or the need to protect the reputation of the school. If it was a 'rearguard action', it was one spurred by a sense of the humane. The statements were a rope thrown to three drowning men. Perhaps Pat Kilroy destroyed the documents because he realized that this rope would not be enough to save them.

36

What did they do, the boys, when they had left Pat Kilroy's office, leaving behind those three signed statements?

Barry Fox caught a bus into town to meet his girlfriend for breakfast. His girlfriend hadn't heard about Conor's death, and Barry didn't mention it. As they walked past the Trinity College cricket fields, Barry stopped suddenly and hooked himself over a railing, bending at the waist. His stomach jumped and gurgled and then coughed up a warm hoard of sputum and bile.

'Hangover,' he said to his girlfriend. 'Last night was fairly rough.'

Stephen O'Brien got a lift home from Richard. He went upstairs and fell asleep. When his mother called him for dinner he came down and ate in silence. Then he went back upstairs and slept for thirteen hours.

Clodagh Finnegan learned about Conor's death from the six o'clock news that night. She immediately rang Stephen, but he had switched his mobile phone off.

When he had dropped Stephen O'Brien at the entrance to his estate, Richard Culhane parked his car in a neighbouring cul-de-sac and let himself panic. He moved the driver's seat back as far as it would go and put his head between his knees and breathed so deeply and so quickly that after several minutes he was afraid his lungs had been indelibly abraded. He calmed himself down by staring at the traffic that passed on the road in view of his windscreen.

Then he went to see Laura.

She was still in her pyjamas. Richard felt a vestigial thrill of desire: vestigial, because he assumed that their relationship had ended and that this would be the last time he would ever talk to Laura.

Laura kissed him and padded morosely into the kitchen. *She knows*, Richard thought. *She already fucking knows.*

He said, 'Did you hear the news?'

'What news? I'm only up,' Laura said.

She made two cups of coffee with the cafetière. Dimly Richard perceived that she was angry with him for fighting the night before. He thought about saying sorry for this, but he knew that it would ring unbearably hollow in retrospect – once he had told her what she needed to know. He longed to be restored to a world in which a day of Laura's disappointment was the hardest thing he would confront.

'I think you'd better sit down,' Richard said. Again he had the strange belief that he was acting in a film – performing, for the benefit of some unseen audience, the details of a story already long familiar.

Laura turned from the cups of coffee and looked at him, registering for the first time the unshaven face, the haggard eyes with their insomniac bloodwork.

'What?' she said. 'What's wrong?'

'Sit,' Richard said.

Slowly Laura sat at the head of the cluttered kitchen table. Richard moved a chair so that he could be as close to her as possible. He found he couldn't meet her eyes. He looked around the kitchen, with its stacked fridge and its glut of gleaming fixtures.

We fucking showed that little cunt.

Richard took Laura's hands and said in a measured voice, 'Conor's dead.'

Laura's tears were noiseless and immediate. They fell from her face and landed softly in an unwashed cereal bowl, mingling with the last of the milk.

'Oh,' she said. 'Oh. Poor Conor.'

There was an interlude of silence: Laura cried silently, and Richard looked at a magnetized ornament that Laura's mother had attached to the door of the fridge. It said: ONLY BORING WOMEN HAVE IMMACULATE HOUSES.

Then Laura looked at Richard and remembered, or seemed to remember, his final, gratuitous kick. She felt an oddly multiform sensation, a mixture of feelings too dense to be examined. Later she would identify this feeling as the sense that many things had suddenly ended.

She put her hand on Richard's face and said, 'You look scruffy.'

'Yeah well I didn't have time to shave.'

'You poor thing.' Laura rubbed her eyes and left a wet grainy smudge of mascara on the back of each hand. 'Did you sleep?'

Richard shook his head.

'When did you hear?' Laura said.

'On the radio this morning.'

'It wasn't your fault,' Laura said. 'It wasn't anybody's fault.'

Pat Kilroy had said the same thing, of course. But Richard had needed to hear it from Laura. And when she said it, and Richard realized that she didn't mean it, that it wasn't true, he was again immersed in a vision of his future – all those visits to important buildings.

'I called Foxer and O'Brien,' he said. 'We went to see Pat.'

Laura began to cry again. 'Oh Jesus. Oh fuck. Conor's dead. Conor's dead. Oh I should call his parents. Oh Jesus.'

'I don't think you should call his parents, babe.'

'Well what the fuck am I *supposed* to do?' Laura stood and began to pace the kitchen.

Richard unrolled a wad of paper towels and offered them to her. She blew her nose and began shredding the damp tissue with her fingers. Richard had already digested the worst: Laura was not surprised that Conor was dead. He tried to remember the fight. How serious had it been, how heavy-handed?

'I just need to think,' Richard said. Then he said: 'I'm sorry. I'm so sorry about this.'

'Well if you hadn't been fucking *fighting*,' Laura said.

He wondered if he should have prepared something to say to Laura. *Sorry, babes, but I think I may have killed your ex-boyfriend.* The humour of this thought emboldened him.

'Well he fucking started it.'

(There is the question of whether Richard or Barry or Stephen

148

were in any sense gratified by Conor's death – gratified, I mean, in the short term, during the day or so following the night of 31 August. *We fucking showed that little cunt*, Stephen O'Brien had said. This kind of triumphalism – brought about by adrenaline, by righteous anger – takes time to fade. The recovery from violent anger, as Richard Culhane already knew, is a period of wilfulness and intractability. The body doesn't easily relinquish such a sense of power and purpose. This would be the physiological interpretation. There is also the moral aspect. Were the boys, even for a day, glad that Conor Harris was dead? Did they think he deserved it?)

'Don't you dare make excuses,' Laura said.

'Sorry.'

Through the kitchen windows the avuncular sun shone, creating golden parallelograms on the terracotta floor.

'He always was', Laura said, 'a stupid fucking cunt.'

She sat at the table and cried. Richard leaned against the counter, thinking, *I did this. I'm the reason she's crying.* He felt bad about this. He also felt affronted. He felt like saying, *I'm the one in real fucking trouble here, Laura. Let's focus on the* real *problem.* But he said nothing.

He knew that getting Laura to address his problems sensibly would take time: maybe the whole day. Nonetheless, he felt a certain amount of urgency.

'I need to know,' Richard said, 'what happened in the club.'

'Nothing happened.'

'Something happened. You walked out with him.'

'I didn't "walk out with him", Richard. He, like, caught up with me. It was a *crowd*, like.'

'We need to get our story straight, Laura.'

'No, *you* need to get *your* story straight, Richard. Conor's *dead.*'

'I *know* that, Laura.'

'This can't be happening,' Laura said. 'This is the worst thing.'

'It was an accident,' Richard said for the first time. 'We didn't mean to do it.'

Laura sniffed and snuffled.

Richard said, 'Where are your old pair?'

'Playing tennis,' Laura said. 'Oh, fuck. I'll have to tell them. Fuck.'

She looked up at him with leaking eyes. 'Do your parents know?'

'My mother knows Conor's dead,' Richard said. 'My dad's playing golf.'

'Who saw it?' Laura said.

'The fight? I don't know. Foxer says, like, twenty people.'

'That was all our *friends*, Richard.'

'It was dark,' Richard said. 'Christ, even *I* can't remember what happened.'

They talked like this for the rest of the afternoon. They talked about what the funeral would be like. They talked about what they would say to the guards if it came to that. They agreed that they wouldn't mention anything to their parents or their friends. They agreed that after today, they would try not to talk about Conor's death at all.

Eventually they went up to Laura's bedroom and lay on the unmade bed. Laura put on some music and turned the volume down. Later neither of them could remember what record she had chosen.

At around five in the afternoon they made love. Richard perceived that, from now on, the few seconds before orgasm would be the only respite he would ever get from thinking about Conor's death. His consciousness was already so embattled, so wholly devoted to the labour of exculpation, that as he lay in Laura's shaded room he recognized something new about his life, a new impossibility: the impossibility of ordinary thought.

Richard stayed in Laura's until ten o'clock that night. After he had left – following a lengthy goodbye of tears and kisses – he stood on the street outside, holding the keys to his car and telling himself that everything would be okay. He could hear the echoing rattle of a ball kicked against the side of a house. The windows he could see were warmly lit, and everything was tranquil. But the sky was turning black, and as Richard walked to his car he could feel a rising wind, tousling his hair and causing the hairs in his forearms to bristle – with cold, with secret knowledge.

Richard Culhane drove home and went to bed.

37

The summer before he died, Conor Harris was working afternoon shifts as a mâitre d' in one of his parents' city centre restaurants. People found this odd. Conor had always seemed to lack precisely the qualities one associates with a host: he was, people agreed, almost quaintly rugged and wild; he was raw and unsubtle. The Conor I remember had the force and sly simplicity of the game he played so well. 'Ah, I know Conor's a bit rough around the edges,' Eileen Harris said once, 'but his heart's in the right place, and that's all that matters at the end of the day.'

Conor did have a great amount of charm at his disposal. Women liked his humour. He seemed childlike, though never innocent. He had a child's frustration with inefficiency or waste. His social skills appeared to be narrow: he was awkward with adults and nervous around small children. These, I notice, are awkwardnesses we associate with adolescence. Conor, of course, was twenty-one years old when he died. Perhaps he was slower than Richard or Laura to abandon that most frustrating of adolescent qualities, that wariness of maturity coupled with a willed dismissal of its opposite.

But he was, it turned out, a very good mâitre d'. Every morning he put on a suit and tie and drove into town. He assumed his post by the bookings table and welcomed people to the restaurant with a deferential smile. He had chosen to work in one of the restaurants that Brendan Harris seldom visited. The family agreed that this was wise.

One afternoon that summer I went in to see Conor at work. He looked like a man I'd never met before. I liked him, then: he seemed to have made some subtle but definite progression, into adulthood perhaps, or into a firmer belief in his own self-worth.

They all had summer jobs that year, of course. The summers in America had been taken care of the year before. Richard Culhane did desultory office work for his father's company of fund-accountants. Stephen O'Brien and Barry Fox were taken on by each other's fathers' firms. That was how it worked.

'You'll make valuable contacts in there, Richard,' Peter Culhane told his son. And Richard did make contacts. He networked. He charmed his father's bosses the way he charmed everyone else: with his looks, his aura of comfort and ease, the sense of ownership that he seemed to seal with a lazy blink as he looked around the office on his very first day, as if to say, 'Yes, this life is mine already; all I have to do is walk into it when I'm ready.'

But the contacts disappeared, the life to which Richard laid such easy claim removed itself from his grasp – not gradually, but instantly: at the moment Conor Harris hit the ground.

38

On Friday, 2 August 2004, Conor Harris ran into Laura Haines outside the Quinn School in UCD. Conor was wearing a Leinster rugby jersey, chinos and sunglasses. Laura wore tracksuit bottoms, Ugg boots, and a Hollister sweatshirt. Because it wasn't term time, neither of them had bothered to dress up: Laura wore no make-up, and Conor had no gel in his hair.

The conversation was awkward.

'Hey,' Conor said.

'Hey.'

'What's up with you? Why are you in?'

Laura held up an armful of nursing textbooks. 'Library. You?'

'Problems with registration.'

(Yet another mystery: neither Brendan nor Eileen Harris could remember Conor encountering any 'problems with registration' in the late summer of 2004. The college confirmed, during the trial, that Conor's bank giro – for the payment of standard fees – hadn't even been sent out by 2 August. So what was Conor doing outside the Quinn School that afternoon? Waiting to see if Laura happened by? Meeting someone else?)

'Will you be playing this year?' Laura asked.

Conor shrugged. 'Hope so.'

Laura looked around: the quiet campus, the summer sun.

'Are you, like, seeing anyone?' Laura asked.

Conor shrugged. 'How's Richard?'

'He's fine,' Laura said. She tried for levity. 'I heard you scored, like, Lisa McKeown.'

Conor blushed – something Laura had never seen him do. She realized that Conor was still in love with her.

'It was just this random thing,' Conor said.

'Well I hear she likes you,' Laura said gently.

Conor said, 'Yeah, well everybody likes me, babe.'

They laughed.

Conor said, 'You going out tonight?'

'Yeah, we're going to Bondi,' Laura said. 'You?'

'Don't know yet. Might go to Harry's.'

'Will Lisa be there?'

'Yeah right. *That's* why I'm going.'

'Listen, Conor,' Laura said. 'Take care of yourself, alright? You're a good guy.'

They embraced and Conor watched as Laura walked away. ('Her ass,' he told me once, 'is, like, *made* for tracksuit bottoms.') She disappeared beneath the concourse, on her way to the library.

The next morning Laura came downstairs to find her mother in the kitchen, brewing coffee in the percolator. On the table was a bag with the BT2 logo on the side.

'Conor Harris was here last night,' said Mary Haines. 'He told me to give that to you.' And she made the sort of face that mothers make, the face that says, *I know what's going on here.*

Laura opened the bag. Inside, wrapped in tissue paper, was a black hoodie, spangled with silver stars.

'Oh my God,' Laura said.

'That's lovely,' Mary said. 'Try it on.'

Laura tried it on. 'It makes me look pregnant.'

'No it doesn't,' Mary said.

Laura went into the living room and examined herself in the mirror above the mantle. She decided that the hoodie did not, in fact, make her look pregnant.

She went back into the kitchen. 'What time was Conor here?' Laura asked.

'About eight,' her mother said.

'Did he stay?'

'No, he wouldn't stay. He's a very polite young man, though.'

'I'm *not* back with him, Mum,' Laura said.

'I never said you were,' Laura's mother said. 'Well? Are you going to keep it?'

'I don't know,' Laura said. 'It cost, like, two hundred and fifty euro.'

Laura's mother made her knowing face again.

'*Stop* it, Mum.'

That afternoon, Laura wore the hoodie to lunch with Richard Culhane.

'This is new,' Richard said, reaching across the table. 'Where'd you get it?'

'My mum picked it up for me,' Laura said. 'I'm wearing it to, like, shut her up.'

Laura, of course, had recognized the hoodie immediately as the one that she and Conor had fought over while they were shopping in Dundrum. She knew why Conor had bought it for her, too. She knew that Conor was apologizing for his behaviour and forgiving her at the same time.

She wasn't sure how she felt about this. Richard's attention had made her uncomfortable about the hoodie. But she never countenanced giving it back or throwing it away.

It wasn't unusual, I should explain, for Richard to remark on Laura's new clothes. All the boys in Richard's group were hyper-observant when it came to how people dressed. But Richard noticed the star-spangled hoodie for a different reason. He noticed it because he had seen it before.

On the afternoon of 2 August – the day before he had lunch with Laura – Richard had been standing outside the Dundrum Town Centre with two boys from his Quinn School class. Richard was waiting for the boys to finish their cigarettes. He looked across the sunlit plaza and saw Conor Harris, standing by the coffee kiosk and holding a bag from BT2.

Impelled by an obscure sense of charity – it was the sense of himself as a victorious suitor – and by the lingering significance of their days on the Brookfield SCT, Richard ambled across to say hi.

'Alright, Richard,' Conor said. 'What's the craic, man?'

'Not too bad, not too bad,' Richard said. 'How's things with yourself?'

'Grand, grand.'

This conversation was no less awkward than Conor's chat with Laura earlier that afternoon.

He and Richard talked for a couple of minutes about the starting line-up for an upcoming Ireland match. Then Richard said, 'What did you buy?'

'Ah, nothing,' Conor said.

'Let's have a look,' Richard said.

(Here it is again, that fixation with clothes so peculiar to these boys and their world. Conor and Richard were like two spoiled princesses, exclaiming over their latest find. But what else could they have talked about?)

Conor opened the BT2 bag and showed Richard the hoodie.

I wonder why he did this, now. He knew that Richard would recognize the hoodie when Laura wore it – that is, if she wore it. But Conor's motives may have been simple. He was trying to cause a fight. He was trying to get Laura and Richard to break up.

'Bit feminine for you, isn't it?' Richard said.

'Well, you know yourself,' Conor said. 'Buying something for the bird's birthday.'

Richard frowned and said, 'Who's your bird, these days? Lisa McKeown, is it?'

'Sort of,' Conor said.

Something darkened at that moment; something passed between the boys that made their faces thicken with remembered mistrust. Was Richard thinking about what had happened all those years ago on Inishfall? Was Conor thinking of Laura, and the way she looked as she walked away from him towards the library?

Richard and Conor said goodbye. Three weeks later Conor would be dead.

I understand, I think, why Laura wore the black hoodie to lunch with Richard the following afternoon. But the question I have to ask is this: Why did she wear it to Harry's Niteclub on the evening of 31 August?

Laura wore the hoodie to lunch because Richard had pissed her off in Bondi the night before.

The Bondi Beach Club in Stillorgan was a themed nightspot. There were three tons of sand strewn around the dance floor, and beach umbrellas and sun loungers. On any given Friday night it would be full of Mounties in bikinis and Rock boys in Hawaiian shirts.

On the night that Laura and Richard were there, the girls who hadn't come in beach attire began, as the night went on, taking off their tops and skirts and dancing in their underwear. Clodagh Finnegan bopped across the dance floor in a red lace bra and cotton briefs. A few minutes after midnight, Richard staggered up to Laura and yelled, 'Get your kit off, babes! Fucking everyone else is doing it!'

Laura shook her head.

'Come on, man!' Richard shouted. Laura could see the capillaries on his nose. 'It's cool, you know? It's just, like, the spirit of the night, like!'

Laura went to the bathroom. A few minutes later Richard apologized and took her home.

So Laura wore the star-spangled hoodie to lunch as a kind of silent retaliation.

In retrospect, all of this – the matter of the star-spangled hoodie – strikes me as both glibly improbable and mercilessly childish. This can't have been why Conor died, surely.

No. Not this. Not this at all.

39

'Have you seen how much weight I've put on?' Laura Haines said to Richard Culhane. 'My tits are getting bigger. I'm like, size 33C but I never had tits this big before.'

This was on 30 August, 2004. Another perfect summer's day. The sky contained a broad tilled acre of fleecy cloud.

It was early afternoon and Laura's parents were at work. Richard lay on Laura's queen-sized bed in nothing but his boxers. Laura was using a GHD to straighten her ash-blonde hair. Richard regarded Laura with seigneurial complacency. He stroked the curve of her hip where it turned into her waist.

He was alert, by now, to what it meant when Laura started talking about her weight.

'Did you have lunch?' he said.

Laura was almost shrill. 'I had a Nutri-Grain bar. *Two* Nutri-Grain bars. That's like four hundred calories. You're only supposed to have fifteen hundred calories a day if you're a girl.'

'You're not fat.'

'I have like a pot belly.'

'No you don't.'

'Yes I do.'

Laura was wearing only a T-shirt. When she stood, Richard could see the inverted trapezoid of whiter skin left unmarked by her visits to the tanning booth. She was perched on the edge of the bed, attending to her hair with one hand and feeling her stomach with the other.

'I wish I looked like Rachel Bilson,' she said.

'You are so much hotter than Rachel Bilson,' Richard said. He sat up so that he could look seriously into Laura's eyes.

This was what Richard enjoyed about relationships. He enjoyed shoring up a girl's confidence about her looks. It was part of the chivalric ideal by which he lived. And he enjoyed hearing about Laura's secret insecurities. Richard's ideal of intimacy wasn't a complicated ideal, but it was subtler than the kind of notions endorsed by people like Stephen O'Brien or Conor Harris.

During Laura's sixth year at Ailesbury College, Richard knew, some of the girls had started to cut themselves. On half-day afternoons four or five of them would disappear into a field beyond the school with a make-up bag full of stolen razor blades and laboratory knives and take turns cutting small incisions into their arms and wrists. One morning Nicola Hennessy cut her wrist so deeply that she was taken away in an ambulance. The girls in their uniforms, grave and respectful, watched her go.

Eating disorders – anorexia and bulimia – were more popular. Girls competed to tell the most convincing lies about how much food they had eaten that day.

'I had a whole Big Mac,' Lisa Corrigan would exclaim as she shivered in a stuffy summer classroom.

'I had a whole packet of digestive biscuits,' someone would say. Or, 'I had this *fantastic* steak last night, *and* we stopped for Abrakebabra on the way home from Bondi.'

The eating-disorder girls were the ones who vomited in toilet cubicles after lunch, the ones who had perfected methods of moving food around a plate to create the illusion of its having been eaten.

Laura was one of these girls.

The school, Laura told Richard, mailed to her parents a packet of documentation a year before she enrolled. A list of requirements for matriculation included *dignity of comportment, a strong work ethic, a sensible approach to dress and behaviour, and an interest in religious matters beyond what is required by mere social convention.* On the cover of the prospectus was a sepia-tinted photograph of the school. *We believe strongly in inculcating our girls with the ethos of the school,* said the letter from the headmaster on the first page.

Laura was a Catholic, too. Laura's Catholicism was one of the things Richard liked about her. He had been proud to take her home to meet his parents.

Peter and Katherine loved Laura Haines. They had already decided that this was the girl Richard would marry. They had thrown a small dinner party for Richard and Laura in early June, and although the subject of religion was never broached directly, enough hints were dropped about Laura's Catholicism to make Peter and Katherine feel secure in allowing Richard to continue seeing her.

I'm talking in this account about people who believed in transubstantiation, in the divinity and Resurrection of Christ, in the teachings of the Pope and in the moral authority of the local parish priest. I'm talking about people who shuddered and clammed up whenever the subject of child sexual abuse in the clergy was raised. I'm talking about people who blessed themselves whenever they passed a church.

There were exceptions to the strictness of their Catholicism, though.

Richard and Laura had had sex, of course, on that afternoon of 30 August 2004, in their customary missionary position. As they lay on Laura's bed, the condom they had used still lay, wrapped in tissue paper, in the waste-paper basket in Laura's en suite bathroom. Although for religious reasons neither of them believed in contraception, they would never have dreamed of having sex without a condom.

That's what I'm talking about. I'm talking about people who were capable of entertaining two wholly contradictory beliefs at the same time, and of perceiving no contradiction.

'What are you wearing tomorrow night?' Richard asked.

'What would you like me to wear?' Laura asked. She coyly twirled the last unstraightened wrinkle of her hair.

Richard knew that this question was not seriously meant. Any answer he gave would have no effect on what Laura decided to wear. This wasn't why he had asked her about it.

'Have you still got that hoodie?'

'What hoodie?'

'The black one. The one your mum bought you.'

'I don't know,' Laura said.

She went into the en suite bathroom and closed the door. Richard put his hands behind his head. He noticed Laura's pale-blue towelling robe hanging from a hook on the bedroom door, the cuffs tucked into the pockets in maternal reproof.

Laura emerged from the bathroom and vanished into the wardrobe. When she came out she was wearing the star-spangled hoodie.

'This one?'

'… Yeah.'

'Do you like it?'

'It's alright.'

'I'll wear it if you want.'

'It won't actually be that cold,' Richard said.

'Whatever.'

Richard said, 'Come here for a minute.'

'Watch the hair.'

Carefully Laura lay on the bed. Richard put his arm around her.

'I love you,' Richard said.

'I love you too,' Laura said.

This was the fourth time they had spoken these words to one another (Laura had kept count), and the second time Richard had spoken them while sober.

They lay in silence for a while, a prone vignette of intimacy and accord. Then Laura said, 'I have a lecture.'

She got up and took off the star-spangled hoodie. Richard said, 'You hear Steve-o ran into Conor Harris the other day?'

'Oh yeah?' Laura said. She looked around for her second shoe.

'Yeah, said he was being a real cunt.'

'Yeah well Steve was probably pissing him off,' Laura said.

Early on the Wednesday morning of that week – the last week of Conor's life – Stephen O'Brien had encountered Conor Harris outside Club 92 in Leopardstown. They had both been drinking. They had a two-line conversation that went like this:

'How's your ma, Conor?'

'Fuck off, Steve.'

Richard Culhane hadn't witnessed this exchange.

'One of these days,' he said now, 'I'm gonna get that bastard.'

'Come on,' Laura said. 'Help me find my other Converse.'

Richard looked up and out of the open window. The last layer of fleecy cumulus had invisibly dispersed. With an unwavering howl of effort, an airplane – at this distance a smoothly mobile point of reflected sunlight – clove diagonally in two the flawless sky.

40

As a matter of routine, one of the nurses in the emergency room called the guards shortly after Conor was brought in. By the time the squad car arrived he was dead. It was the guards who woke the Harrises at 6 am to tell them that they'd lost their son.

'Are you the father of Conor Harris?' the guard said as he stood in the hall of the house in Donnybrook. Beyond the open door Brendan Harris could see dawn light and chalky shadows.

'Yes,' Brendan said. 'What's he done?'

But Brendan Harris already knew that Conor was dead.

Eileen was still in the bedroom, looking from the window at the emergency numbers on the side of the white-and-yellow Ford parked in her driveway.

An hour later the garda press office released a short statement about the incident. They confirmed that they were treating Conor's death as suspicious. They appealed for witnesses to come forward. That this appeal was never answered – that no one was willing to speak, that the guards had to track down their various witnesses over the course of almost a month – remains a point of difficulty for various people.

Another, more controversial point of difficulty is the fact that there had been a squad car in Blackrock on the night that Conor died. People had seen the fluorescent syncopation of its lights as it cruised along the main street and out towards Dun Laoghaire at around 3 am. The guards have always maintained that they saw no evidence of a violent incident in progress at this time. The Harrises, in private, have considered pressing this point, arguing for a charge of criminal negligence. This was during the period when they were ready to consider prosecuting anyone and everyone, including the bouncers employed by Harry's Niteclub, in the hope of finding some redress, some compensation.

My own belief is that the squad car passed Harry's Niteclub far too early to have done anything about Conor Harris.

The two bouncers who worked the door at Harry's, I suppose I should explain, insisted to gardaí and journalists that, although they had seen the fight, they had agreed that it was taking place outside what they called their territory, the notional six-metre semicircle that extended around the door of the club, beyond which they were not supposed to go in the defusing of a violent incident. So they did nothing. And then they went home.

Conor's death was the third headline on RTÉ radio's morning news programme: twenty-one-year-old man dies after being kicked and beaten outside a Dublin nightclub. Barry Fox's father heard the story and registered the name of the club. He tried Barry's mobile and left a voicemail message that Barry heard only later, after he had already heard the news from someone else.

As far as I've been able to ascertain, Barry Fox's father was one of only three people directly involved in the case who learned about Conor's death from the radio that morning.

The other two people were Katherine and Richard Culhane.

In the hours following the identification of Conor's body in St Vincent's Hospital, the gardaí took brief statements from Brendan and Eileen Harris and from Conor's older brother. They established who Conor had gone to the club with (Fergal Morrison) and who he was likely to have encountered there (this was mostly guesswork on the Harrises' part: a ragbag list of remembered names, among which was the name of Laura Haines).

The Harrises hadn't been particularly alarmed when Conor failed to make it home on the night of 31 August (or the morning of 1 September). He often stayed overnight in a friend's house. Brendan and Eileen had in fact assumed that Conor would stay at Fergal Morrison's.

Fergal Morrison was the one of the first people questioned about

Conor's death. He had left the nightclub early with a St Anne's girl. They had gone to Eddie Rocket's and then he had taken her in a taxi to her home in Dalkey, where, for half an hour or so, they had 'made out' on the couch of her family's living room. Fergal was reticent about the details of this half-hour – understandably: the girl (her name was Joanna Carruthers) was seventeen years old, and Fergal, at this time, was twenty-two.

The officer in charge of investigating Conor's 'suspicious' death was Detective Sergeant Michael Feather, a red-faced Tipperary man who had been educated at Clongowes Wood. He visited Joanna Carruther's house in Dalkey and established that Fergal Morrison had, in fact, been on her couch at about 3 am.

Privately Fergal told me that he had spent most of this half-hour trying to persuade Joanna to have sex with him. She offered a compromise in the form of a blow job. So at the moment Conor received his third and final kick to the head and his brain was irreparably damaged, Fergal Morrison was getting his cock sucked by a seventeen-year-old girl in low-rider jeans and a pink string top from BT2.

(I think about this often, this question of simultaneity. What were we all doing at the moment of Richard's kick – at the moment of the kick we all assume to have been Richard's? Eileen and Brendan Harris were asleep. So were the Culhanes and the O'Briens. It happens that Laura Haines's mother was awake, boiling a kettle for coffee in the striplit kitchen and watching some foxes in her back garden. In that sense, Laura's mother had the drop on the rest of us: she was an insomniac *before* Conor died. The rest of us took a night or two to catch up on our sleeplessness.)

Detective Sergeant Feather extracted from Joanna Carruthers a list of people she knew had been in Harry's that evening and who might possibly have stuck around long enough to have witnessed the fight. It wasn't a long list. It became clear that all of the girls Joanna named were in her year at St Anne's College, Foxrock. Although they were technically underage, most of them had been taken to the club by their college-age boyfriends. Detective Sergeant Feather hoped that these boyfriends would eventually start to look like a shortlist of suspects.

I don't know what led Michael Feather to emphasize the private-school aspect of the case from its inception. Perhaps his own experiences as a Clongowes boy told him something about our world. In any case, he knew from early on that Conor's death had not been the result of a mugging, because Conor's wallet was still in the pocket of his jeans when he arrived in the emergency room.

Eileen and Brendan Harris were intractable in their mistrust of Michael Feather. This began, I think, in the hospital, when Brendan asked for Conor's effects and the garda gently explained that these would have to be kept as evidence. Eileen Harris would blame Michael Feather's incompetence for the eventual overturning of Richard Culhane's manslaughter trial. But by this time Eileen was blaming everyone, because she could find no obvious target for her anger.

In fact Michael Feather was thorough and methodical. He was a moustachioed man with a large, block-shaped head, who suffered from a stammer that afflicted him only on words that began with the letter H. It took the form of a peculiarly toneless repetition of the initial syllable. 'I'll ha-ha-have to speak to you about this at the ha-ha-house,' he would say in his rustic monotone.

'He's doing it on purpose,' Eileen Harris would complain. And indeed, the stammer seemed deliberate; it lacked the embattled quality of a true impediment.

I trusted Michael Feather. In his press conferences he was circumspect, even boring. He gave very little away. And he did find out who killed Conor Harris, even if it took him almost a month.

Eventually the guards contacted the principals of the southside private girls' schools and asked them to take the names of any students who had been in Harry's on 31 August. This produced a slightly longer version of Joanna Carruthers's list. So Michael Feather's team began the business of calling on all of these girls in their houses in Stillorgan and Killiney and Dalkey and Ranelagh and Milltown and Mount Merrion and Shankill and Blackrock and Donnybrook and asking them what they'd seen.

All over south County Dublin girls were surprised on September evenings at their homework by uniformed guards with notebooks and questions. Most of them enjoyed the drama, I think. For a couple of days at St Anne's it became a point of pride to have been visited by the gardaí. Girls who hadn't yet been interviewed prayed for the opportunity to air their own particular theory about Conor's death. Most of what the guards uncovered consisted of improbable speculation. Several girls – I knew them, vaguely – had decided that the source of the argument (and everyone was sure there had been an argument, even the people who had seen nothing, who had been too drunk to pay attention) was a girl – specifically, Laura Haines, whom every one of these private-school girls knew or had heard about.

There was a problem of age. Most of the girls who were interviewed at this point in the investigation were three or four or five years younger that Conor Harris and his peers. So they had only the most tenuous of links to what had actually happened in Blackrock that night. It took the guards some time before they could identify the people who knew Conor directly.

But eventually they ended up visiting Laura Haines.

It wasn't Michael Feather who paid the call. If it had been, maybe Richard Culhane's name would have come to the attention of the Director of Public Prosecutions rather sooner than it did.

Laura was interviewed by a uniformed female guard whose male partner sat silently in the kitchen and looked around as though he had never seen a house like this before. Laura had been studying for her first radiology exam of the academic year. On the black marble of the breakfast counter her textbooks lay open. There was also a ring binder, a pencil case coated in burgundy fluff, and a cup of tea, now cold.

'And were you at this Harry's nightclub on the night of August 31st?' the guard asked Laura.

'Yeah, I was,' Laura said.

'Did you see anything that you think might help us find out how Conor died?'

'No,' Laura said. 'I came home early. By myself. I had a headache.'

'How did you get home?'

'My boyfriend took me. We got a taxi.'

'And what's your boyfriend's name?'

'Richard.'

'Surname?'

'Culhane. His name is Richard Culhane.'

'And what time did he take you home at?'

'It was, like, two o'clock in the morning.'

When the gardaí had left, Laura went upstairs to her room and asked God for forgiveness.

The guard who questioned Laura was not aware that she had once gone out with Conor Harris. Michael Feather knew this, obviously: he had learned about Laura during his talks with Brendan Harris. But the information hadn't trickled down to the cops who did the routine interviewing. So what happened was this: in over forty interviews, Richard Culhane's name surfaced only twice. In Laura's interview, it might as well have never been mentioned at all.

Yes, Laura Haines lied to the gardaí to protect her boyfriend. She acted, she later claimed, out of a conviction of Richard's innocence. This was a lie, of course. Laura knew Richard was guilty, and she knew he would be caught. Her lie was a delaying tactic. She needed to keep Richard's guilt to herself long enough to find out if he was sorry.

Laura Haines, remember, was the only person who saw the fight in its entirety. She was also the only person who understood why it happened and what it meant.

I'm surprised that Laura's lying to the guards didn't become more central to the case. The lawyers involved chose not to make an issue of it. Richard's refusal to come forward – this became an issue. But Laura was never charged with obstruction of justice. She was never seen, by either the defence or the prosecution, as anything other than a material witness.

I find this strange. I find it strange because I know (or suspect) how Laura feels about Conor's death. She feels that, although she never threw a punch, she is as responsible as Richard and Barry and Stephen and the various anonymous others who joined in the fight for the fact that Conor died.

The details of Laura's interview went largely unnoticed in the incident room that Michael Feather had established at Donnybrook Garda Station. It wasn't until Detective Sergeant Feather spoke to Debbie Guilfoyle, Dave Whelehan's girlfriend, that he procured a list of suspects.

Eventually the gardaí assembled almost eight hundred statements about the events of 31 August 2004. But Debbie's was the one that closed the case. She cried as she told the guards about the fight. She said she could only remember three people who were near Conor at the moment he fell.

Stephen O'Brien.

Barry Fox.

And Richard Culhane.

The boys were arrested at 7 am on the morning of 25 September 2004.

PART THREE

Heavy Damage

41

Once, from the window of a coach that was taking the Brookfield Senior Cup team to a training session in Kildare, Richard Culhane had a vision of hell. They were passing through a council estate, a promontory of damp grey pebble-dashed houses, rows of them, in the middle of a treeless plain of sickly greensward. For a moment Richard was oblivious to the gaudy shouts and howling of his team. He was gripped by what he saw. Two girls in pink tracksuits pushed matching buggies, their faces narrow and strained, as though, Richard thought, they had just sucked on something sour. There was graffiti on the houses and on the crumbling boundary walls. Men stood around in dispirited cliques, their clothes dirty – it was obvious even at this distance. In a flickering instant Richard had a vision of an alternate self: a self condemned to live out a short and desolate life on this barren ground, a self trapped by a pregnant girlfriend or a financial holocaust, a self with no choices, no future.

It caused him some anxiety over the following months. He imagined he had been given a glimpse of the worst possible course his life could take.

Of course, we never see the actual failures that await us, the failures that surprise us by being at once so banal and so lurid. We never foresee failure's power to ruin, insidiously, not simply the rude outline of a life – the sturdy trajectory of school–college–career–marriage–retirement – but the miniscule, auxiliary things, the pleasure we take in a pop song or a game of rugby.

Have I mentioned that, after Conor's death, Richard never played rugby again? This hasn't been remarked upon in the popular discourse, perhaps because so few people are aware of it. But it's true: he stopped playing. He has never, as far as I know, spoken aloud about why this might be.

Eventually, everything in Richard's life was poisoned by its actual or potential association with the thing that had destroyed him. In the year after Conor's death he found he couldn't read any book that mentioned death, or watch any film that contained a scene set in a nightclub.

There was nothing he could think about that didn't lead him inexorably back to that night outside Harry's in Blackrock.

In the warm house in Sandycove that smelled of lavender and furniture polish, Richard watched as the pleasure was drained from his life. He accepted it, I think.

He thought it was only fair.

42

On the morning of 25 September Michael Feather questioned the boys in a small interrogation room in Donnybrook Garda Station. First he let them wait in separate cells. Then, one by one, he sat them down at the cratered wooden table with the tape deck and the notepad and asked them, in his oddly stilted and formulaic stammer, about 31 August.

In the words of one reporter, Barry Fox and Stephen O'Brien coped 'extremely badly' with this first brief imprisonment and with the interrogations that followed. They sweated and cried. They muttered things like, 'This isn't fucking fair,' and, 'We had nothing to *do* with it, man.'

Later, in private, Stephen O'Brien admitted that he had assumed that he would never be arrested. 'Things like that just don't fucking happen,' he said. What he meant was, *Things like that don't happen to people like me.*

Richard was calm – unusually so. Because of this Michael Feather, during those first few hours, pegged Stephen O'Brien as the ringleader. (It wasn't until the Laura Haines connection surfaced that Richard assumed his proper status.) But Richard was calm because he had anticipated all of this: the whitewashed cells, the smell of disinfectant in the corridors. He knew his tour of important buildings had begun.

The boys had solicitors present during their questioning, of course. As soon as Richard drove away in the squad car, Peter Culhane had called a family friend named Gerald Clinch, who arrived at Donnybrook Station at 11 am and who was sitting beside Richard when Michael Feather asked his questions.

Gerald Clinch was a nervous little man, brimming with thwarted love for the world, aggressive when he meant to seem passionate, scathing when he meant to seem kind. Gerald had done a law degree at UCD and then got his parchment at Blackhall Place in Dublin. He wore grey suits with gold cufflinks in the shape of small harps. He slapped Richard hard on the shoulder and told him that everything would be absolutely fine as long as Richard told the truth about what had happened.

What seemed to matter to people later on was that Gerald Clinch and Peter Culhane had been at Brookfield together. They had both been on the SCT.

Barry and Stephen shared a solicitor named Peter Mason, who had agreed, at Maurice O'Brien's request, to defend both his son and his son's friend.

Mason was a Merrion boy. A joke about him became famous, during the trial: he was said to have been the only member of his SCT who could carry a bucket of water across the field, hung from his erect penis, without spilling a drop.

Many phone calls were made that morning, as the boys waited in their separate cells. Peter Culhane rang people he knew: people who worked in the Department of Justice, people who worked for Fianna Fáil, people who worked for law firms and medical-insurance firms and tax-accountancy firms. He wanted to find out two things. He wanted to find out if he could get Richard off the hook, and he wanted to find out how much it would cost if he couldn't.

Brendan Harris heard about the arrests on the radio and called Donnybrook Garda Station. He had known that arrests would be made, but he hadn't known who the culprits would be. His first response, when he heard Richard's name, was to say out loud to the empty kitchen, 'I knew it.' As the day wore on, he began to wonder what exactly he had meant by this.

Barry Fox's father rang Maurice O'Brien, who was also calling barrister friends and political cronies. (Do I need to point out, at this late stage, that everyone Peter Culhane rang had gone to Brookfield and that everyone Maurice O'Brien rang had gone to Merrion Academy?)

'Don't worry,' Maurice said. 'We'll sort this out.'

People began to say this all the time: *We'll sort this out*. People said it to Richard and Stephen and Barry. They said it to Peter and Maurice. They said it to Eileen and Brendan Harris. There were variations: *We'll sort this whole thing out* and *This whole thing will be sorted out* and *We'll get this sorted, don't you worry*.

Gerald Clinch and Peter Mason said it to the boys: 'We'll sort this out.'

They were friends, Clinch and Mason. They'd gone to UCD together.

Michael Feather spoke to Richard first. Richard said he thought Conor Harris had thrown the first punch but Richard didn't know why the fight had started. He said that he himself had been peripheral to the fight. He admitted his own involvement but he said it was minimal. He said he couldn't remember Stephen or Barry being involved but he conceded that it was possible they had been. He said he had had a lot to drink but that he hadn't become aggressive. He said he was deeply sorry that Conor had died and that he deeply regretted his involvement in the incident. He insisted that he was innocent of Conor's manslaughter.

During all of this Gerald Clinch rapidly clicked a retractable ballpoint and nodded narrowly in waltz time.

Stephen O'Brien was next. He explained that Conor had been acting aggressively in the moments that led up to the fight. He insisted that his own involvement was peripheral. He confessed that he had thrown the occasional punch but that the fight had been so messy that it was hard to work out who had done what to whom. He said he had had a lot to drink but that he hadn't become aggressive.

During all of this Peter Mason wrote on a refill pad in a small neat script.

Then it was Barry Fox's turn.

Barry admitted he had been one of the people who kicked Conor in the head as he lay on the street. He said he was certain that

Richard Culhane had been involved in the fight from the very beginning. He didn't know who threw the first punch either, but he said he thought it might have been Richard. He said that Richard had been drinking heavily all night and that he had become aggressive. He said that Stephen O'Brien had been the first person to jump into the fight when it began. He said that he had wanted to call an ambulance for Conor but that Richard had convinced everyone to leave.

During all of this Peter Mason shifted about in his seat and wrote furiously on his refill pad.

None of the boys mentioned the statements taken by Pat Kilroy. None of them mentioned *We fucking showed that little cunt*. None of them mentioned that Richard's current girlfriend had once gone out with Conor Harris.

By this time Mick Conroy, the taxi driver against whose idling vehicle Laura Haines had slumped, had come forward offering to help the gardaí. Michael Feather supervised a line-up during which Mick Conroy identified Richard and Stephen as the boys who had been doing most of the kicking and punching outside Harry's. Mick Conroy did not identify Barry Fox, who stood in the same line-up. This would be cited as a mitigating factor by Barry's barrister at the trial, and would be one of the reasons that Barry's sentence was eventually shortened on appeal.

When Barry's first interrogation was over Gerald Clinch and Peter Mason spoke swiftly and privately in a corner of the busy station. Naturally they have never disclosed the substance of their conversation.

Then Richard and Stephen were questioned again. They confirmed certain minor details of Barry's story but denied having kicked Conor or having become aggressive due to drink.

When these interrogations were over Michael Feather sat back and said to himself, 'Well, I think we ha-ha-have them there.'

Of course the boys had been unable to confer with one another about the details of their stories. Richard and Stephen had trusted that Barry's version of the night's events would broadly concur with their own.

Barry had cried a good deal during his interrogation. When he went back to his cell he sat on the thin grey mattress of his cot and examined his feelings. For a moment he felt relieved, lightened of a burden. Then he remembered the statements that Pat Kilroy had taken and kept in his office safe. He realized that Richard and Stephen had probably not been compelled – by conscience or anxiety or fear – to confess. He saw what he had done. He saw Richard and Stephen and himself and their long shared future of whitewashed rooms and public failure.

He leaned back against the wall and said, 'Fuck it.'

The arrests featured in most of the next day's papers. The articles all said the same thing, more or less. They said this: 'Three students appeared before the Dublin District Court today, charged with man-slaughter and violent disorder. They are accused of killing Conor Harris, 21, outside Harry's Niteclub in Blackrock, on August 31st. They replied "Not guilty" to the charges and were released on bail, to appear again in court at the end of the month.'

Time to go.

43

After the arrests, everything began to change. The boys had been about to begin their third year at UCD. Now they had to defer their places. Richard felt numb as he filled out the forms. He was sure – though he couldn't have told you how he knew – that he would never go back to the university again.

And he was right. He never did go back. Neither did Stephen O'Brien or Barry Fox. For a few weeks Peter Culhane talked about sending Richard to Cambridge to resume his studies, 'when all this has blown over'. I don't know what became of this plan. Maybe Peter still entertains it, maybe it's one of the things he brings up every now and then in the big white house on Inishfall.

Every morning, while they waited for the trial to start, Richard went into the garden and met the refusing stare of the empty swimming pool. Peter had had the water drained because the pool's upkeep was costing him too much money.

The worst thing about Richard's guilt was how utterly it had arrested him in time. He knew that his real existence had ended at the very same time that Conor's did, in the very same heartbeat. Now Richard was a ghost in his own life. Sometimes, in the middle of the night, he began to fear that he *was* a ghost, quite literally: not his own ghost, not the ghost of Richard Culhane, but the lingering spirit of Conor Harris.

And it would follow him, comprehensively, this stasis, this guilt. When he turned sixty-five he would still be the boy who killed Conor

Harris. When he shuffled into the nursing home, he would still be the boy who killed Conor Harris. When he died himself – he increasingly felt – he would just be catching up.

Although the pool was empty, Richard still found consolation in staring down at its leaf-strewn tiles. He thought that Peter had been right to drain the pool. There was something indecent about its slap and shimmer, some quality of luxuriousness that none of them felt they deserved any longer.

So for half an hour or more every morning Richard Culhane stared into an empty swimming pool as if trying to descry his future.

And what were the Harrises doing, during this period of procedural quiescence?

Eileen Harris had taken to making ever larger patchwork quilts. She no longer attempted to sell the results. She assembled a small library of pattern books and a chaotic archive of scraps and frayed samples. She sat in the kitchen of the house in Donnybrook and sewed patches together. I don't think any of the quilts she began were ever finished.

Brendan Harris watched television. He had left the running of the restaurants in the hands of his executive assistant, and now that he had nothing to do all day, he sat in the living room and watched television for hours, shrunken in the armchair like a very old man. He had constantly to remind himself that Conor was dead. Mourning, he thought, must be a state of appalled recognition, continually renewed.

It seemed to him that he had already lived through his whole empty future.

One day Father Connelly called on them.

'I wanted to offer my condolences,' he said as he stood on the doorstep in the rain.

Brendan Harris had answered his ring. Eileen appeared at his shoulder.

Conor's brother came down the stairs.

'Fuck off,' Conor's brother said, and closed the door in Father Connelly's face.

44

Katherine Culhane's mother, who had suffered all her life from a nameless pain (undiagnosed, untreatable), eventually became so introverted, so reluctant to leave the house in Stillorgan and finally the bedroom, that Katherine had grown slowly sure that she too would end up housebound in middle age, sighing and shifting behind veils of cigarette smoke, so beset by auguries and terrors that she would be unable to walk past the gate at the end of the garden. By the time of Conor's death, it hadn't happened. Katherine had done a decent job of suppressing the more outlandish of her hereditary anxieties. She was known as a sprightly and personable woman. She wrapped presents for the Vincent de Paul at Christmas. She kept it together.

All of this changed once she found out that her son had killed Conor Harris.

How did Richard tell her? I find myself wondering. Did he sit her down in the kitchen with diffident gravity, holding her chair with that inbuilt politeness for which he was famed? Did he let the knowledge trickle through, via hints and gestures? Did he rely on the six o'clock news to get the conversation started? Or did Peter and Katherine find out only when the jacketed detectives knocked on the painted lumber of their fine front door, looking for their only son?

Picture the Culhanes, standing in the kitchen with the stubbled and deferential guards, staring at Richard as he confirms – with a nod, with his silence – what the guards have said. He wouldn't have to have said or done anything incriminating, in the legal sense.

Katherine, intuitively, would know what her son had done. And she would have been amazed by how much love she felt for him; astonished that her first instinct, in the face of such horror, was to cherish him, to clutch him to her breast and tell him he was already forgiven. But that is what heartbreak feels like: it feels like more love, at first, because love is always trying to become pain, as though pain were its fulfilment.

To Katherine, Richard was still the duffel-coated child (buttons painfully undone) that she had deposited in the bare yard on his first day of primary school. Richard, strange to say, had been an anxious child. 'Mith the buth!' he had lisped as a two-year-old, during the days before the Culhanes had been able to afford two cars and Katherine had brought him into town on one of the old green double-deckers. 'Mammy! Mith the buth!'

In the year that followed her son's arrest Katherine Culhane grew more and more like her mother. The meals she cooked became more elaborate, as her mother's had. Now, every day, she served up three-course meals culled from cookbooks, as though, in hiding from the world's complexity, she needed to create private elaborations, little domestic practices over which she had demonstrable control. She seldom left the house. She hired a Nigerian maid named Namwali to pick up her shopping every week, and when Namwali arrived with her carload of plastic bags, Katherine would insist on inviting her in for camomile tea and homemade cranberry muffins with ice cream. And Katherine would listen with terrible patience as Namwali told her hard-luck tale: emigration, poverty, isolation, abandonment.

Katherine noticed that Namwali always sniffed as she entered the house, as though performing a quick olfactory diagnosis of the hall, the living room, the kitchen. Katherine came to find this wariness vaguely reassuring.

Katherine took up smoking again. She stayed in bed until noon and spent the rest of the day padding around the house in her dressing gown. One afternoon she noticed dust on the bottles and cases of make-up that stood ranked beneath her bedroom mirror. She found that the house, in which she had taken such pride, had become merely a place in which to suffer, somewhere to remark on the glacial progress of ordinary pain, measured, it seemed, in millimetres of unvacuumed dust, in streaks of unscrubbed urine that turned the toilet bowl the colour of a sun-bleached newspaper.

She found it impossible to speak to Richard. He seemed to spend most of his time in the long back yard, staring down at the surface of the pool, which by now, with autumn well advanced, was full of fallen leaves. Katherine watched him from the kitchen window, unable to approach his shrunken frame. A psychiatrist – hired at Peter's expense – had told them to keep Richard on a kind of informal suicide watch. And so Katherine watched him, listlessly, inattentively. She knew that her son would never commit suicide. It was worse than that. He would live, he would endure, hauling around his burden, his curse, the curse that condemned the rest of them, too, the curse that meant the agonizing end of their beautiful family. Whenever she came upon him in the kitchen or the conservatory – holding one of the cups of coffee he spent all day making and never drank – she would flinch, and this craven gesture, unwelcome and unwilled, came to stand for her relations with the rest of the world. She flinched often, now. She flinched when she turned on the television, when she opened the big front door.

Nonetheless, she read the newspapers, looking for news about the case. She conferred hopelessly with solicitors. And, obsessively, she debated with herself the nature of Richard's crime.

She wondered if what Richard had done was a sin, whether in the eyes of the Lord Richard was guilty of some profound and damnable offence. But if it was a sin, she reasoned, calmly working through the logical equation, then what kind of sin was it? Not a sin of omission, surely, because Conor's death hadn't been brought about by inaction, by neglect. Then perhaps it was a sin of commission: Richard's kick had killed Conor Harris. But he hadn't meant to kill. So it wasn't a sin of commission, either. Perhaps it wasn't a sin at all.

But it felt like a sin. It felt like a sin she had committed herself. It left the same hollow, fretful afterglow. She might as well have been there on the night that Conor died.

I wonder if she thinks about this still, Katherine Culhane, if this is what she cries about, out there in the big white house on Inishfall.

45

According to one newspaper, 'the manner of Conor Harris's death caused widespread revulsion and shock' among his fellow students and friends. This revulsion and shock initially took the form of whispered conversations around the dinner table. Then it took the form of silence.

According to various newspapers, Brendan and Eileen Harris were 'distraught' or 'inconsolable' or 'tearful and deeply shocked'. They made 'heartfelt appeals' and 'stinging attacks' and 'desperate pleas'. They were 'strong in the face of grief'.

(Of course, they were not strong in the face of grief. They were felled, defeated, harrowed.)

According to other newspapers, the Culhanes 'stood staunchly by their son'. They were 'determined to prove his innocence'. They were 'deeply saddened' by Conor's death but 'one hundred per cent certain that Richard had not been involved'.

According to various newspapers, Conor Harris was 'kicked to death by a mob'; 'brutally assaulted by a gang of drunken youths'; 'tragically killed during an altercation outside a nightclub at three in the morning'.

According to various newspapers, Richard and his friends were 'snobs' or 'rich kids' or 'rugger-buggers'.

According to other newspapers, Richard and his friends were 'students' or 'former private-school pupils' or 'three young men of college age'.

All of these descriptions are true at a certain level.

The Unique Selling Point of the story – from the point of view of the news media – was, of course, the private-school element.

People called up radio phone-in shows and explained that Brookfield boys and their ilk were thugs and always had been, and that it was about bloody time they got their comeuppance.

Other people said that this was a tragedy and we should be thinking of the families involved instead of airing our private grievances.

Still other people said that fights like the one in which Conor was killed happened every night on the streets of the capital, and that the news media had only seized on this one because the people involved were rich and educated and therefore glamorous in a way that other violent young men were not.

Still other people opined that the boys would get away with it because of who they were and where they'd gone to school.

About the night itself people were less passionate but equally opinionated. Some people said Conor must have been asking for it. Other people – echoing the girls of St Anne's – said that there must have been a woman involved.

I don't think anyone ever expressed the opinion that Stephen, Barry and Richard were innocent.

It's interesting that these debates were conducted almost entirely through public channels. It's also interesting that the people who wrote to the newspapers and spoke on the radio and on the television about the case were not people who had grown up in south County Dublin. They were northsiders or people from the country.

On the southside, we were expected to be quiet.

All over south County Dublin people tacitly agreed that the case would not be publicly discussed. Of course, almost everyone in south County Dublin either knew Richard or Stephen or Barry or Conor or their parents directly, or they knew someone who did.

So on the southside the kids continued to do what they had always done. They went to rugby games and hockey matches and they went shopping for Debs dresses and tuxedoes (this was September–October, after all, Debs season), they went out drinking, they went to school and church, they did their homework.

In telling this story I am breaking the pact of silence that was our unanimous response to the arrests. People have told me that this story would be better left untold, that in telling it I will merely cause more suffering, more grief. But this story is all I have. My motives in telling it have been purely selfish, and have had nothing much to do with propriety or with the need for good manners. In this account, subjective and partial though it must inevitably be, I'm talking about people who need to be talked about. I'm talking about people who think pain and grief are things you should bury, people who fear and despise the public airing of sorrow, people who have no sense that stories are our simplest – perhaps our only – way of talking about the things that hurt us. I'm talking about men and women who try to live as though suffering was something that happened to other people, never to them.

These are my people. I love them, for what it's worth.

46

This story is too hard to tell.

But I can't escape it now, not yet.

Nearly there, nearly there.

Soon I'll go away, I think, to that cramped and rainy island in the lonely west. Soon I'll leave for Inishfall.

47

Two weeks into the trial Peter Culhane woke up at four o'clock in the morning, panicking and covered in sweat. His left arm was paralysed and his chest was tight and sore. He stumbled along the landing to the room where Katherine slept.

'I'm having a heart attack,' he said. 'I can't breathe.'

Katherine was immediately awake. She called an ambulance and waited with Peter in the kitchen. He sat in the yellow light clutching his chest and breathing loudly.

'I was dreaming,' he said. 'I dreamed about Richard.'

'Shh,' Katherine said.

Richard was in his room upstairs. He wasn't asleep, though the family's GP had prescribed him some heavy-duty tranquillizers. He listened as the ambulance arrived and took Peter away. Peter and Katherine had an argument in the driveway about whether Peter should go to the hospital alone. 'You stay with him,' Richard heard his father say. 'You need to get him to court.' When the ambulance had gone he heard his mother walking slowly up the stairs. She put her head around the door of his room.

'Your father's gone into hospital,' she said.

'I know.'

'It's probably stress.'

'Yeah.'

'Are you sleeping, at all?'

'A little bit.'

'Alright, so. I'll call you in a couple of hours.'

It was probably stress, the doctors in the emergency room said, once they had taken Peter's blood pressure and checked his lung capacity. 'Are you under any great strain at the moment?' they asked.

Peter nodded.

'We'll keep you in for observation, anyhow. Just to make sure.'

Peter knew some people at Vincent's. They gave him sleeping pills and a bed in a semi-private room on the third floor. In the twilit quiet of the hospital Peter lay wide awake. He suspected that the sleeping pills were placebos. From the neighbouring bed a white-haired woman stared at him, unsleeping. Peter sat up and put on the trousers Katherine had hurriedly packed for him.

He was worried about the media. What if the papers found out he was here? For Peter this was the most painful aspect of the case, more painful even than the certain knowledge that his son had been involved in the death of another young man. There was something obscene about the fact that his family were constantly appearing in the papers, on the television. And what was worse, they were constantly linked with the O'Briens and the Foxes, as though they no longer possessed an individual identity, as though all three families were somehow the same. *Richard wasn't like those other boys*, Peter thought. *Richard had something, a nobility.*

On the radio during the week Peter had heard a woman say, 'Richard Culhane is nothing but a thug. You can dress it up all you want but that's what he is, a thug.'

And Brendan Harris kept saying to the press, 'My son was murdered and I want his murderers punished in a court of law.'

Peter Culhane was an old-fashioned man. And he was a Brookfield boy. This means that he had sentimental notions about honour and propriety.

He had discovered that he hated his son almost as much as he loved him.

Richard had hardly spoken to Peter since the beginning of the trial. They said hello when they passed on the stairs. That was it.

Two weeks before, someone had sent an anonymous envelope to the house, addressed to Richard. It contained an old-fashioned magnetic tape of a song called 'Gary Gilmore's Eyes' by a band called The Adverts. Gary Gilmore had been a murderer in the seventies, Peter remembered. He threw the tape away and burned the envelope before Richard could find it.

Richard went out into the back garden every morning now and stared into the empty swimming pool.

One by one, the little things were being taken away from them.

Katherine had spent most of her time over the past year buying paintings for the living room. She liked to buy paintings by up-and-coming Irish artists who painted soothing watercolour seascapes or forested hills. She had also paid for a *catalogue raisonne* of her small collection to be printed and laminated. She left the catalogue on a sideboard in the living room, so that visitors could identify the paintings that hung there.

But there weren't visitors anymore, not as such. Just lawyers and priests and, very occasionally, Pat Kilroy, who came at times when he thought it unlikely that he would be noticed by the press.

'I've caused enough controversy already,' Pat would say as he accepted a cup of tea and a scone from Katherine.

Peter was grateful for Pat Kilroy's continued support. But the real truth of things, he knew, was that his family was alone, consummately alone. All they had left was each other.

The pain in Peter's chest had gone away. He got into his shirt and shoes and went downstairs to the ER.

Peter knew that this was where Conor Harris had been taken on the last night of summer, 2004. This was where he had been pronounced dead.

Peter walked out of the ER and down to the Rock Road. He hailed a passing taxi and asked the driver to take him to Blackrock. By now it was six o'clock in the morning and the dawn light was visible in the east, out over Dublin Bay.

It was very cold.

At Blackrock DART station Peter paid the driver and climbed the steps that led to the sea wall. He stood on a bridge that crossed the tracks. The first trains would begin to run in a few minutes. They came into the station more quickly than you expected. Warning signs told you to stand behind the yellow line.

On the other side of the bridge was a short shingly beach. Waves came in at deafening volume. We hear more acutely in the early mornings, Peter knew. We're more used to silence, less prepared to screen out the noise of the day.

The waves came in and drew away, came in and drew away. They reached for the shingles and came away with nothing.

The tracks began to vibrate with the approach of a train. It sounded like snapped whips, or a steel cable, dangerously uncoiling. The train was coming out from town. People were waiting on the platform beneath.

Peter looked at the sea and he looked at the tracks.

He thought about his son.

Richard had something, a nobility.

Was it possible that Richard *wasn't* different? Was it possible that he was just like the other Harry's Niteclub boys? That he was just like Stephen O'Brien and Barry Fox and Conor Harris? That there was nothing between them, no way to tell them apart, nothing to distinguish any of them from the others?

Harry's Niteclub, closed now and boarded up, was a two-minute walk from the station, Peter knew. Harry's Niteclub, where his son had beaten Conor Harris to death.

He climbed down from the bridge, went into the DART station, paid for a ticket with the change in his pockets, and rode the train out to Dun Laoghaire station.

48

On a Wednesday morning in late April 2005 Laura went to see her counsellor. This was three weeks into the first of the trials. She sat in the waiting room of Dr Reid's office in Ranelagh and looked at the paintings that hung on the walls. The walls were painted beige: Laura knew that places like this were always decorated in calm and soothing colours. The paintings themselves were somnolent watercolours of seascapes, sailboats, sand dunes.

Laura's parents, by now, were 'deeply concerned' about Laura's mental health. It troubled them that they could find no outward index of her pain. She was eating normally, driving into college every day, even going to the cinema with her friends every Friday night. But Brian and Mary Haines remembered how Laura had felt after her grandmother's death. They remembered how she had acted when the family dog was put down. They had come to depend on her weekly visits to Alison Reid – the last visible evidence that Laura was upset, and also, paradoxically, the last visible evidence that she was willing to do something to make herself better. The visits cost a hundred and thirty euro per session. Spending money, Laura perceived, made her parents feel happier. Spending money made Laura feel happier, too, but she was not eager to admit this.

Dr Reid showed Laura into her office.

'Well,' she said, folding her hands on her lap. 'How are you holding up?'

Laura shrugged. 'How do you think?'

'I'm not sure how I'd be holding up, under the circumstances,' Dr Reid said. She let an interval of silence pass before she said, 'Are you eating?'

'Yes,' Laura said.

'How much?'

'Like, two meals a day.'

'Of what would those meals consist?'

Laura shrugged again. 'Whatever my mother gets up off her fat arse and manages to cobble together, I suppose.'

'Do you feel hostile towards your parents at the moment?'

Laura shrugged.

'It's alright if you do, Laura,' said Dr Reid. 'Those feelings are perfectly normal.'

'You're always telling me my feelings are normal,' Laura said.

'Do you think they aren't?'

'How could they be? I mean, this isn't exactly a normal fucking situation to be in, is it.'

'What isn't normal about it, Laura?'

'My boyfriend is on trial for, like, murder. Is that normal?'

'As I understand it, Richard is on trial for violent disorder.'

'Yeah but we all know what that means.'

'What does it mean?'

'It means he killed Conor.'

'And do you think he did?'

Laura shrugged. She noticed that Alison Reid's skirt had begun to collect little balls of excess wool. She said, 'Where did you get your skirt?'

'I can't remember,' Dr Reid said.

'Figures,' Laura said.

After a moment Dr Reid said, 'Is there anything *you* want to talk about, Laura? Anything particular on your mind?'

Laura sighed and looked at the floor. Again there was a space of silence.

She had decided that what she missed most about the life she seemed to have left behind was the public aspect of going out with Richard: arriving at parties together, savouring the fact that everybody paid attention to the tiny jokes and gestures that they shared, the signs that marked them out as a couple. Now when they were together they were always alone, in Richard's bedroom. Their sex had become frowningly serious. Once, halfway through, Laura had begun to cry, and Richard had continued to pound away at her, grunting softly in anger or embarassment.

Then she said, 'I used to go to these parties when I was in school. This is like, fifth or sixth year. And all the guys would take turns punching each other in the face. They had a name for it. It was called, like, the Punch-Face game.'

'Was it a fight?'

'They weren't fighting. It was some game they'd invented. One of them would punch the other in the face as hard as he could. Then the other guy would punch the next guy in the face as hard as he could. And so on around the room.'

'Then what did they do?'

'They compared bruises.'

'Were they being macho? Were they showing off for the girls?'

'No. You don't get it. It was just what they did.'

'Did Richard ever play this game?'

'Yeah. But this was before we started going out. Once he got this black eye that lasted for, like, two weeks. It turned totally yellow and then he had to tell his mum where he'd got it.'

'And how did you feel about that? About Richard playing the punching game?'

Laura shook her head. 'It doesn't matter how I felt about it. It doesn't matter how I feel about anything. It just matters that it happened. And that's what you have to deal with.'

49

On a Tuesday morning, just before his trial was due to start, Richard Culhane drove to an ATM in Sandycove and withdrew six hundred euro, the maximum that could be withdrawn in a 24-hour period, from his student bank account. Then he drove out to the airport.

It was 7 am. Richard stood in the middle of the long check-in area and looked up at the Departures board. He had wanted to go to America, but he knew the flight would be too expensive. It was a pity. America was a familiar quantity. He would know what to expect there. But it would be too expensive and he would only be able to get a ninety-day tourist visa.

That morning he had gone into Katherine's bedroom and taken his passport from the safe in his mother's wardrobe.

He had formulated no plan that would take him beyond the drive to the airport. But there was a bleak nobility, he thought, in driving along the half-empty motorway in his small car, a hastily packed Brookfield sports bag beside him on the passenger seat.

He looked up at the Departures board.

London, Paris, Milan.

A police warning would probably come up when they scanned his passport. He was awaiting trial. The gardaí had told him not to leave the country.

Leaving the country without telling anyone was the nearest Richard could come to committing suicide.

He couldn't commit suicide, of course. He believed it was a sin.

Malaga, Montreal, Birmingham.

It was also possible that he would be recognized. His picture had been on TV and in the papers a lot over the last few days. He was surprised to find that fame felt like being contaminated. But he wasn't famous, was he? He was something else.

People had begun sending hate mail to the house in Sandycove. There had even been death threats, which made Richard angry. Didn't these people understand? It had been an *accident*. Nobody had *planned* Conor's death. It was just a stupid mistake.

Berlin, Helsinki, Moscow.

Richard watched a young couple with their two young children. The kids were sitting on a baggage trolley and their father was pushing them along. Richard wondered where they were going.

'Mum!' one of the boys kept shouting happily. 'Mum!'

Richard looked up at the Departures board.

There was only the long drive back to the house. That was all there would ever be.

He went back outside to pay for his long-term parking.

50

On the first morning of their trial for manslaughter and violent disorder, the boys arrived early, wearing black suits that their parents had bought them for the occasion. 'It's like the opposite of a Debs,' Stephen O'Brien said as they waited in the Four Courts vestibule with their legal team.

'BAD DAY IN BLACKROCK', said a headline on that first morning. Every front page proffered a brief recap: the kicks, the ambulance, the arrests, the schools.

The day was brightly cloudless and the early cold had receded from the glare of the sun. Across the cobblestones tight-lipped, sombre men hurried with dark leather briefcases.

Richard wondered why police stations and courts – buildings in which so many extreme and complicated emotions were endured – were always so unbeautiful, why they were so dirty, so wearily drab. But perhaps things were meant to be this way; perhaps our lowest feelings deserved no better than these empty rooms with their institutional paint and standard-issue furniture. Nothing, after all, is more boringly institutional, more cheaply standard-issue, than suffering.

They entered the court with their heads down. Cameras were forbidden inside the chamber proper, but as the boys passed over the threshold they provoked a seizure of clicks and flashes and whirrs.

In the gallery were four blonde girls with swept-back hair and tangerine make-up. They waved and called, 'Hi, Richard!' Richard didn't recognize them. Once, girls had called his name from the sidelines of a rugby pitch. He had always known their names.

(These four girls had taken the morning off school and come to the first day of the trial to see Richard, because they thought he was 'gorgeous'. That evening their parents forbade them from going to the trial again.)

The three boys sat at the front of the court, at the same table as Gerald Clinch and Peter Mason. Stephen O'Brien had heard that if you spent your days in court writing things down, then people would think you were actively working to prove your own innocence. So he spent the whole trial scribbling on a refill pad. Once, Richard managed to get a look at one of Stephen's pages. It said *Stephen O'Brien Stephen O'Brien Stephen O'Brien* over and over again in the same blocky script.

Barry Fox took the proceedings personally, and often leaned across to ask Gerald Clinch or Peter Mason what was going to happen next. His heavy shoulders rose and fell with the tidal dramas of the trial.

Richard said nothing. He hardly moved. He sat and looked at the wall directly in front of him. This had the effect of making him seem deeply and unalterably alone.

The Harrises were in court every day. Every day they struggled through the throng of agitated newsmen and took their seats in the gallery – two padded school chairs in the front row, preserved every morning with squares of folded cardboard marked HARRIS. I never found out who put these markers there. But everyone respected them. Everyone in the gallery stood aside to let the Harrises wriggle by.

By this stage the Harrises had turned Conor's room into a guest bedroom. But there were never any guests to stay in it. For some weeks their lives revolved around the trial. They were earnest publicists for their own bereavement. They gave interviews and made statements. They wanted to make sure that people knew how they felt.

Every morning and afternoon, Eileen and Brendan Harris shuffled past Peter and Katherine Culhane without speaking.

Outside the court, for almost every day of the trial, was a gaggle of protesters and onlookers, gawkers and well-wishers, the curious and the prurient. These were the people who appeared on television vox pops, who provided 'colour' for newspapers and radio reports. Among them, on several occasions, was Father Connelly, in clerical vesture. He was keen to stress that God loved all of His children equally, that Richard and Barry and Stephen were no less favoured by the Almighty than Conor Harris had been.

Some people found this point of view distinctly odd.

Jury selection for the Harry's Niteclub trial had taken slightly longer than was usual, because of the perceived 'high profile' of the case. But twelve men and women had been agreed upon, selected for their objectivity, their poise. I scrutinized them as they squirmed and mumbled in their steep enclosure. According to the newspapers, only two of them were from Dublin. I applauded this. Other people did not. Other people felt that a certain amount of provincial incomprehension would be inevitable when these country folk were confronted with a case so deeply bound up with a Dublin way of life – with a southside way of life, a private-school philosophy, a ruling-class worldview. But there was nothing anyone could do about this now.

The trial judge was a different story. Mr Justice Brendan Harrington was a private-school boy, a former rugby hooker and King's Inns graduate, a southside native and father of two exemplary St Anne's girls, a man who owned a Rover and a jeep and who lived in a house with a wine cellar and a heated jacuzzi. He sat on the bench and regarded the courtroom with saturnine contempt. Although trial judges were discouraged from fraternizing with legal counsel under any circumstances, Brendan Harrington was familiar with the lives and bright careers of Peter Mason and Gerald Clinch. He had been to school with one of them, and he had been to university with both.

In short, Mr Justice Harrington was a Brookfield boy.

It has been suggested that Mr Justice Harrington should have excused himself from his duties for the duration of the trial, that some other judge should have held the gavel while Richard and Stephen and Barry were in the dock. But what was the alternative? Most of the Dublin judiciary had been educated at Brookfield or Merrion or Michael's or Gonzaga or Blackrock. What were people supposed to do?

'OLD SCHOOL TIES DOMINATE COURT PROCEEDINGS', ran one headline, underneath a photograph of some students dressed in the Brookfield colours, waving red-and-white scarves outside the court.

That first day, in his opening statement, Peter Mason asked the jury to consider the prior good behavior of the three accused. He pointed out that the manslaughter charges with which they were faced were simply not supported by the available evidence. He asked the jury to remember that up to six other young men had been involved in the Harry's attack, and that his clients had been only peripherally involved. He reminded the court that all three boys had entered pleas of Not Guilty to charges of violent disorder and manslaughter.

(*Manslaughter.* A peculiarly vivid word, more vivid perhaps than *murder.* It conjures a casual bloodthirsty proficiency, as though the slaughter of a man were simply all in a day's work.)

The prosecution insisted that Conor Harris had been the victim of a vicious and unprovoked attack, and that in denying culpability, the Brookfield boys were attempting to evade justice.

But the evidence was ambiguous and everyone knew it. The state felt that it could safely place the boys at the centre of the fight. It could tentatively assign to them responsibility for the kicks that led to Conor's death. But accounts differed and the boys pled Not Guilty and the medical evidence couldn't prove who had done what at what point in the fight.

The trial lasted for three weeks. I was there every morning and afternoon.

Mick Conroy testified. When the prosecution asked him to identify the two boys he had seen outside Harry's Niteclub – the two boys he had already chosen from a line-up in Donnybrook Garda Station – he pointed to Stephen O'Brien and Richard Culhane. He said he had no memory of Barry Fox's involvement in the fight.

Pat Kilroy testified. The prosecution made much of the secret statements he had taken on the morning after the incident, but Kilroy was staunch in maintaining that these statements corresponded in every particular to the statements taken from the boys at the time of their arrest. He said the boys had always been 'of the highest character' and that he was proud that they had been educated at Brookfield.

Laura Haines testified. Everyone expected her to cry, but she was stoical. She told the court that Richard had not been the one who threw the fatal kick. Richard, she insisted, was barely involved in the fight by that point. When the prosecution asked who, in Laura's opinion, *had* been involved in the fracas at the moment the fatal kick was delivered, Laura said she was unable to recall.

A St Anne's girl named Aoife Farrell testified. Of more than a hundred witnesses questioned by the murder squad, she had been closest to the fight when it occurred. 'Conor was defenceless,' she said. 'He just fell down hard and, like, his hands were down by his sides while they were kicking him in the head.'

'And did you see Stephen O'Brien or Barry Fox or Richard Culhane deliver any of these kicks?'

'Yeah,' Aoife said. 'All of them did, I think.'

Debbie Guilfoyle testified. 'I don't think it was Richard who did the kicking,' she said. 'He was, like, too far away.'

'But you said that perhaps a dozen young men were involved in the fracas at this point.'

'Yeah, like maybe ten or twelve.'

'And did you see Richard Culhane walk away from the altercation at any point?'

'At the end.'

That was what they called it at the trial: the fracas, the altercation.

The state pathologist testified. He was on the brink of retirement and testifying at the Harry's Niteclub trial was almost the last thing he did in his official capacity. 'In my opinion Conor Harris died from swelling of the brain and inhalation of blood due to multiple facial injuries.'

'And what caused this swelling of the brain?'

'In my opinion the swelling of the brain was caused by repeated blunt force trauma.'

'For example, three kicks to the head?'

'In my opinion the injuries would be consistent with three kicks to the head. I could locate three points of impact consistent with that explanation.'

The boys themselves testified. They all said the same thing: minimal involvement, Conor started it, not sure who did the kicking.

When Barry Fox was asked if he had indeed kicked Conor in the head – as he had said during his first interrogation – he said, 'I may have. I don't remember.'

Three weeks into the trial, Mr Justice Harrington announced that the evidence as it stood would not support a charge of manslaughter against any of the boys. He directed the jury to consider the charges of violent disorder only.

The jury was absent for sixteen hours. During that time the Harrises gave a television interview in which they expressed their sadness and confusion about the manner in which the manslaughter charges had been dismissed.

'What does it take, to find justice in this country?' Brendan asked.

The jury came back and said that they had found all three boys guilty of violent disorder. Controversially, they recommended that Richard Culhane be tried for manslaughter.

Mr Justice Harrington quelled shouts and cries from the public gallery.

Magaret Harris began to cry and was consoled by Brendan.

Mr Justice Harrington sentenced Barry and Stephen to nine months in prison. In view of Richard Culhane's 'probable role in instigating this fracas and of therefore precipitating the death of Conor Harris', he was sentenced to a year in prison. Mr Justice Harrington instructed the DPP to prepare a file for Richard's manslaughter trial.

When the verdicts had been handed down, Eileen and Brendan Harris were asked to provide what was called a Victim Impact Statement. On the day that Brendan Harris read this statement to the court, the vestibule and the car park outside were filled to overflowing with journalists and camera crews and 'members of the public'. In his three-page statement, Brendan Harris insisted, as he had insisted all along, that his son had been murdered, and that the convictions for violent disorder that had been brought against Barry Fox, Stephen O'Brien and Richard Culhane were laughably inadequate. He also stressed that an unknown number of other young men had not come forward to confess their involvement in Conor's death. For he and his wife, Brendan said, sleep had become a thing of the past. Their lives had been irrevocably altered. They wanted not vengeance, but, simply, justice. They sought redress for their son's untimely death. That this had not proved possible, Brendan Harris felt sure, would be for the Harrises a source of unending sorrow.

Outside the court a gaggle of protesters shouted, 'There's no justice!' as Richard and Barry and Stephen were bundled into the windowless van.

Peter Mason and Gerald Clinch were already organizing their appeals.

51

Laura visited Richard while he was in prison, not as some tabloid Bride of Frankenstein (and there were newspapers that took this angle), but rather as a sort of Florence Nightingale figure, which by then I think Laura had decided she was. Our generation are dying to be victims or carers. Laura thought she was both. But she thought Richard was the bigger victim. She thought he deserved compassion from somebody.

I could address, at this juncture, the question of Laura's loyalty. But what would be the point? She stuck with Richard. That's what happened. Why bother to puzzle over her motives?

Clodagh Finnegan didn't stick with Stephen O'Brien. In the week that followed the arrests she went around telling people how fucking weird it was that her boyfriend had been, like, arrested for murder. When it became clear that Stephen and the other two boys would go to trial for their involvement in Conor's death, Clodagh stopped replying to Steve's texts and phone calls. Eventually she rang him and said, 'Eh, I don't think this is working out, Steve-o. You know what I mean, like.'

Barry Fox's girlfriend – they had never been particularly serious – didn't last much longer.

And they lost their friends. At Brookfield it had always been skirting impropriety to raise the subject of the Harry's Niteclub crew. Now that the boys had been found guilty, everybody clammed up. Nobody recalled aloud Richard's triumphs on the pitch. Nobody brought up any stories involving Barry or Steve. The silence – voluntarily assumed, of course – was total. The silence was so total that even Richard and Stephen and Barry were aware of it, as they settled down on their sagging cots for their first night in gaol. They knew that nobody from Brookfield would ever speak their names out loud again. They knew that that beautiful world, the world of nights out in Blackrock, the world of Senior Cup teams and perfect houses and tolerant parents, was closed to them forever.

Yes, they lost their friends: and this was probably the thing they found hardest to take.

So Stephen had only his parents to visit him in prison.

Barry had only his father.

Eileen and Brendan Harris were doorstepped by a reporter and asked how they felt about Laura's visits to Richard in prison. They said nothing. But I think it just confirmed what they had been feeling all along: that they would receive no sympathy from anyone who was there on the night Conor died. The event had by then become so irreducibly complex, so resistant to straightforward analysis, that anyone who had actually been there when it happened found themselves hopelessly mired in ambiguity whenever they tried to reconstruct the night.

Richard was in prison for eleven months – his sentence was shortened for 'good behaviour'. For the first three weeks he was kept on suicide watch. His shoes had no shoelaces, his prison-issue trousers had no belt.

The Harry's Niteclub boys were kept in the minimum security wing. Richard had been terrified at the prospect of winding up in a cell with a pockmarked, strung-out junkie from Tallaght or the Liberties. When he realized that he would be allowed to spend much of each day in the prison rec. room, far from the cells where they kept the hardcore element, he thanked God.

He shared a cell with a young man named Micko who had used an unloaded sawn-off shotgun to rob an off-licence. When Micko's sentence was over Richard shared a cell with a drug dealer named Buzz. It turned out that Buzz had sold weed to several of Richard's friends.

Whenever she went to the prison Laura would queue with all the other visitors – all the teenage mothers with their buggies and prams – until she was admitted to a large room full of cheap tin tables, at one of which sat Richard Culhane in his olive-drab prison jumpsuit.

Here was Laura Haines, Ailesbury College girl, wearing her €200-make-up, her Abercrombie shirt with the collar turned up, her American Eagle sweatpants with the logo across the ass; here was Laura Haines, with her silver earrings and her pendant silver crucifix, her car keys in one hand and her mobile phone in the other, stepping into a room full of the smell of unwashed bodies, picking her way through the squalling children and the tattooed men until she found her way to Richard's table.

And Richard? Richard knew he was in the last of the important buildings. There would be no more importance, ever, not for him.

Every morning the hero of the Brookfield SCT shuffled into the rec. room in his poorly fitting jumpsuit and stared at the television until it was time for some perfunctory exercise. The first time Laura visited him she was staggered by his faceful of stubble; she had never seen Richard with a beard before. He let it grow. There was, he thought, no point in trying to look good. Who that mattered, after all, would be seeing him now?

Richard spent most of his time in prison trying not to think about things. He tried not to think about, for example, the fact that Peter Culhane had cried when Richard was accepted to study at UCD. He tried not to think about what his parents might be doing during his sentence – though he already knew: they were hiring ever more expensive lawyers to sift through the evidence, trying to find out if there was a way to get Richard off the hook that he was already so plainly impaled upon. He tried not to think about who Laura might be seeing, who she might be talking to.

(She was seeing me. She was talking to me.)

Laura sat opposite Richard at his cheap tin table. Their conversations always went the same way.

'How're you doing?' Laura would ask.

'Alright. People keep trying to sell me drugs. Not the hard stuff. Just, like, weed and shit.' Richard looked around. 'Like, 90 per cent of the people in this room are doing drug deals right now.'

'I know.'

'So, have you heard anything about Foxer and O'Brien? How're they doing?'

'Okay, I think.'

(The boys, I should explain, were in three different prisons. Of their nine-month sentences, Barry Fox and Stephen O'Brien served five months each.)

'Yeah,' Richard said. 'I bet they're fine.'

By now, Richard had hated Barry and Stephen for a long time. And they had grown to hate him, because they blamed him for being the one who delivered the fatal kick and made them murderers, instead of just kids in a fight.

52

A month before the second trial began and ended, Eileen and Brendan Harris took a holiday. Brendan drove them down to Kinsale, County Cork, where he had booked a room in a large hotel on the busy seafront. He had got the room at an out-of-season rate.

They drove in silence, with the radio off.

Most of the rooms in the large hotel were empty. On the way to the restaurant for dinner on their first evening they passed a disused conference room with a view of the bay. Sheeted tables gleamed in the half-darkness. Chairs were stacked in the dusty corners. Through the shaded picture window Brendan saw a tanker leave the bay.

The restaurant was operating at a reduced capacity. A waiter in a threadbare tuxedo told them that they could have the beef or they could have the fish, but everything else was off because the summer chef had left. They ordered the fish.

'This is disappointing,' Eileen said, meaning the food.

'It's alright,' Brendan said. Food all tasted the same to him now.

Photographs of the Harrises had been appearing (or reappearing) in the papers: photos of them at Conor's funeral, photos of them at Michael Feather's press conferences, photos of them on the street outside their house. On the way down from Dublin Brendan had stopped for petrol and glimpsed in the garage's service station a row of tabloids trumpeting some fresh reports about Richard Culhane. They kept using the same picture of Richard, the blurred one from his student card.

Brendan and Eileen had stopped reading the newspapers.

After dinner they took a walk along the seafront. Brendan, who had been to Kinsale before, had expected the little marina to be full of yachts and sailboats. But the place was empty.

'They've all left,' he said to Eileen.

'It's freezing,' Eileen said.

They went to bed. Eileen read a book – a paperback romance – while Brendan flicked through channels on the television. One channel piped in the soundless feed from a security camera stationed at the end of the marina. Brendan left this on and stared at it: the black water, the empty dock.

He lay awake beside Eileen, who was also lying awake, until the alarm went off and they could legitimately begin another day.

53

People still think a deal went down between Gerald Clinch and Brendan Harrington. 'That's the way this country works,' people will tell you. 'The old boys' network. Clinch goes up to his old school pal and says, 'Sure these lads are our kind of people, Mr Justice. They went to Brookfield. You know that boy's death couldn't have been their fault. We'll do a deal. Let them off the hook and I'll make your life a little bit easier.'

I think this is a naive interpretation.

Brookfield boys do not do 'deals'. They don't talk out loud about what they want, least of all to each other. They don't promise each other favours in exchange for a good turn here or there. That isn't how it happens. It happens in silence. It happens without conscious effort. It happens because that is how it has always happened. *We'll sort this out.*

But the old boys' network, if that's what you want to call it, can only do so much. It cannot, for example, organize the forgiveness of the community. It cannot absolve you of your sins. It cannot give you back the life you've lost.

Barry Fox's sentence was shortened on appeal. So was Stephen O'Brien's. Richard served eleven months. And then there was the question of the manslaughter trial.

In the period that interposed itself between the convictions for violent disorder and the manslaughter trial, a new state pathologist took up his post. The Director of Public Prosecutions, for reasons that have never become entirely clear, asked him to provide a new report on the post-mortem data assembled after Conor's death.

In this new report the state pathologist opined that Conor's injuries were 'relatively minor', and that his death had probably occurred as a result of 'injuries and alcohol'.

Richard's manslaughter trial was stillborn. The criminal proceedings never made it into court. The DPP entered a *nolle prosequi* and the trial judge (a Gonzaga boy) formally declared the case abandoned.

This was the last time I saw the Culhanes, marooned on the steps of the Four Courts, their exit barred by the ranks of journalists and TV cameras. Richard had just been released from prison. It was a morning in early autumn: the sweep and crash of crisping leaves, the lingering filigree of fine frost on garden grass. Was Laura hanging around that day, I wonder? I didn't see her there. But I wouldn't be surprised to find that she had come out to watch Richard make his exit from the public sphere.

Inside the vestibule Richard had made a brief statement for the cameras. 'I would like to reassert that I was not responsible for the death of Conor Harris. I was fully prepared to mount a complete defense against these charges of manslaughter. I am an innocent man.'

There were boos and catcalls from the restive crowd.

Peter Culhane asked that his family be allowed to peaceably resume their lives. He asked that the media 'do the decent thing' and leave them be.

Eventually the bailiff shouldered a path through the crowd and the family were able to leave.

The Harrises left without speaking to the media.

The crowd outside the Four Courts shouted things like 'A mockery of justice!' and 'One law for the rich, another for the poor!' These cries were taken up by a number of columnists and editorial writers. Pundits and interested parties began to say that the problem was larger than the machinations of a few private-school past pupils. They began to say that the flaw was systemic, that the country's legal institutions were hidebound, or riddled with incompetence, or archaic, or corrupt.

After a week or two, the story died and was replaced by something else.

And that was that.

But it isn't the trial or the 'miscarriage of justice' or the old boys' network or even Richard Culhane in prison that I keep thinking about, that I keep going back to, helplessly, again and again. What I keep going back to is the night itself, the night of 31 August 2004, the night about which so much has been publicly written and secretly said. What I keep going back to is the night that Conor died.

54

For Richard Culhane, the night's drinking started early, and this would be a problem later on.

Richard met the lads in Stephen O'Brien's house in Dalkey where, in the massive living room at 5 pm, they cracked open their inaugural cans of cider. This was a ritual: the first can was always chugged, and the last to finish had to buy a round when they got to the club. In this case, Barry Fox was the loser. He was subjected to a brief round of masculinized derision. Then, this first hurdle having been cleared, everyone opened their second can and started to relax. This early drinking was what counsel for the defense would later call an aggravating factor. And the people who started drinking earliest were Laura Haines, Barry Fox, Stephen O'Brien and Richard Culhane. By pulling strings with their parents, all of them had managed to get the afternoon off.

At 5.30 pm Conor Harris got home from work and, still wearing his suit and tie, ate dinner (a lamb curry, cooked by Eileen because Brendan had been missing all day, supervising a new menu at the flagship restaurant).

The last thing Conor said to his mother was, 'See you later, Mum.'

I am struck afresh by the banality of this.

During the initial stages of the investigation, the guards were keen to establish whether any of the boys had taken drugs on the night of 31 August. Everyone knew that Stephen O'Brien had taken, in the previous few months, to smoking the occasional spliff – 'You'd fucking *have* to, going out with Clodagh Finnegan,' as Laura put it. But counsel for the prosecution established to the court's satisfaction that none of the boys were stoned or stoked or mashed or high when they set out for Harry's Niteclub. Of course, by the time they were arrested, it was too late to do bloodwork on Richard, Stephen or Barry. Several newspapers opined that it would be unusual if the boys – including Conor – had *not* been on cocaine or ecstasy when the fight broke out, the consumption of illegal narcotics being in the nature of the youth of today. But Richard and Barry and Stephen and Laura all swore that they hadn't touched anything stronger than booze that night. I believe them. Richard and Laura were reflexively puritanical about drugs. That this didn't stop them getting shitfaced on a weekly basis is just one more contradictory aspect of their characters, just one more thing I find I can't explain.

At 6.10 pm Clodagh Finnegan arrived at Stephen O'Brien's house, and she and Laura disappeared upstairs to get ready. The boys could hear squeals and giggles from the bathroom. At one point Laura came downstairs to the living room, wrapped in nothing but a purple towel, to find the charger for her mobile phone. When she left Barry Fox told Richard that he was a lucky bastard.

And Richard *felt* like a lucky bastard, on this last evening of his real, untroubled life. He experienced the kind of desultory composure that came with knowing that, whatever happened that evening, he would be somewhere near its heart, monitoring, recording, cajoling. Laura was part of this, too. She would be – of this Richard was scornfully certain – the most beautiful girl in the club, the girl that everyone wanted to fuck. This kind of pride is not a complicated feeling, but it is a profound one: the pride of sexual possession.

Between 6.00 pm and 7.30 pm (when the girls were ready to leave), Richard, Stephen and Barry drank five cans of cider each. Before they left, everyone necked a double-shot of Bailey's, a bottle of which was at that time the sole occupant of the O'Briens' living-room liquor cabinet.

Richard leaned into Laura's ear and told her in a whisper that her dress was the hottest thing he'd ever seen her wear.

'Hotter than my Debs dress?' she asked.

'Just a bit,' Richard said.

Richard had been disappointed by Laura's Debs dress. It had been a white gown tricked out in lacy frills. To Richard's consternation (even though he and Laura had never even kissed when he took her to her Debs), the dress concealed Laura's cleavage.

The gang prepared to leave the house.

Around this time someone – I've never been able to find out who – rang Barry Fox and informed him of a change of plan: instead of going straight to Harry's, the gang would convene at the Queen's Inn in Dalkey 'for a quick one before everyone heads to the 'Rock'.

Barry explained this to Stephen, Richard and the girls, all of whom were very drunk.

'Cool,' Richard said. 'Harry's will be fucking shit until after eleven, anyway.'

At 7.50 pm Conor Harris left the house in Donnybrook. He had showered and shaved, and gelled his hair. He had debated with his mother about bringing a jacket. By now the warmth of the sun had failed and given way to a gathering evening cool. But you didn't bring a jacket when you went to Harry's: the queue for the coat room would be huge, and it cost a fiver to check things in.

Laura Haines had discussed this problem with Clodagh Finnegan as she straightened her hair in Stephen O'Brien's bathroom. She had brought an extra-large handbag – large enough to contain the star-spangled hoodie that Conor had given her, in case she got cold later on.

It's safe to say that Conor was experiencing a certain amount of anxiety as he travelled on the number eleven bus into the city centre. The plan was that he and Fergal Morrison would meet Lisa McKeown and her 'best friend' – a St Brigid's girl named Caroline Smyth – in Café en Seine on Dawson Street. Conor was fine with this. But Fergal had mentioned that 'everyone' was going to be in Harry's that night, and that he was keen to join them. 'Everyone', to Conor Harris, meant Laura and Richard.

What was the state of Conor's relationship with Laura Haines on 31 August?

They hadn't spoken since their meeting outside the Quinn School on 2 August. Conor had been half-expecting a thank-you text from Laura, telling him she loved the hoodie. But she had said nothing, and Conor had had enough time to become embarrassed by his gesture.

There was also the usual anxiety, the inverse of what Richard Culhane felt as he contemplated his beautiful girlfriend in Stephen O'Brien's massive living room: the anxiety that, whatever happens, you will *not* be at its centre, that your social supremacy ended with your graduation from secondary school, that your life will never offer such intensity again.

At 8.00 pm (they had stopped at a garage so that Laura could buy smokes), Richard and the boys arrived with their primped and polished girlfriends at the Queen's Inn.

Barry Fox paid for a round of whiskeys – and a Malibu and orange juice for Clodagh Finnegan.

The beer garden of the Queen's Inn was full of boys who had gone to Brookfield or Merrion Academy, and girls who had gone to Ailesbury College or St Anne's. In other words, it was full of the people that Richard Culhane had known for most of his life. Again – although now the feeling was adulterated by drink, and by the mild competitive aggression that always accompanied the social proximity of the graduates of four Dublin rugby schools – Richard felt a familiar complacency.

Clodagh Finnegan told a rambling story about vomiting on her hair extensions at a party.

Richard and Barry engaged in casual raillery with some Merrion Academy boys.

'It's gonna be a good night, lads,' Stephen O'Brien said, raising a glass.

'Legend,' Clodagh Finnegan said.

Dave Whelehan arrived. He and Stephen manfully embraced. Dave bought a round of drinks.

Richard registered complacently the admiring looks that Laura drew from boys and girls alike. He took her to a quiet corner of the beer garden and spent a short time kissing her.

Richard looked around and saw Carl Cox and Jason Freeman and Liam Byrne and Simon Stapleton and Brendan Doherty and Michael

Reddy and Ronan Toomey and Colm Kennedy and Fionn Doyle. He saw Debbie Lonergan and Jodie Regan and Kelly Finn and Aoife Walsh and Ciara Fagan. He had played rugby with or against every one of the boys and he had scored or slept with most of the girls.

All of these people would later end up in Harry's Niteclub in Blackrock.

In Café en Seine on Dawson Street Conor Harris ordered his first drink: a Diet Coke. He wanted to be sober when Lisa McKeown arrived.

According to the coroner's report – the first, contested coroner's report – Conor's blood alcohol on the night he died was consistent with his having consumed four or five pints over a period of about six hours. In other words, he didn't start drinking until he got to Harry's. And remember: he was a stocky guy, a former scrum half for the Brookfield SCT. The point of this is that he wasn't drunk. He wasn't flat-out falling-down hammered. I saw Conor drunk. After five pints you wouldn't have noticed any change in his behaviour. He could handle his booze.

So could Richard, generally speaking. But by the time he got to Harry's, he had had an awful lot to drink.

At 9.20 pm Conor, Fergal, Lisa and Caroline stepped off the DART at Blackrock station and walked the short distance to the door of Harry's Niteclub. The bouncers sized them up and let them in.

Conor had planned to spend the evening gently flirting with Lisa McKeown, but as soon as she had arrived he had become unaccountably depressed. The plan had been that Conor would act as wingman while Fergal pursued Caroline Smyth. But it turned out that Caroline had a boyfriend in America – 'Fucking boyfriends in America get all the fucking hot birds,' Fergal complained to Conor while the girls were in the bathroom. Conor decided that he would take it easy on the drink and go home early.

This changed later, when he saw Laura Haines arrive on the arms of Stephen O'Brien and Barry Fox.

At 9.45 pm Fergal Morrison got chatting to a St Anne's girl named Joanna Carruthers. Conor did his best to entertain Caroline and Lisa. He told them some rugby stories. The girls giggled and told him he was a rugger-bugger. Conor told the girls that if he was a rugger-bugger then they must be rugger-huggers. This was an old joke. Conor wasn't using his best material. He didn't see the point.

The club was a crammed and sweaty miscellany of mobile flesh. You had to wait at the bar for twenty minutes before anyone would serve you drinks. People were buying their pints in batches of two or three so they wouldn't have to queue. The music made impossible any conversation but the most straightforward. Conor and Lisa and Caroline were shouting at each other. Eventually Lisa gave up and dragged Conor on to the dance floor.

At 10.30 pm, following a rowdy DART journey, the Dalkey gang arrived outside Harry's. The bouncers sized them up and started selecting.

Richard didn't make the cut.

'Sorry, mate,' the bouncers said. 'Too drunk. No way.'

'What the fuck, man?' Richard said. 'Come *on*. Do me a favour.'

'No chance.'

The bouncers told Stephen and Barry and Laura and Clodagh and Dave that they could go inside. Richard's face was flushed and his heavy shoulders worked.

'Give me a *break*,' he said. 'I've only had a couple of cans, like.'

'Yeah, right,' the bouncers said. 'Sorry. No can do.'

'*Fuck*,' Richard said.

For a moment the people behind Richard in the queue thought that there was going to be a fight. But Richard swore loudly and stepped away from the entrance to the club.

His friends went in without him.

It was not uncommon, in those days, for Richard to bribe his way into a nightclub. He would slip the bouncers a fifty and his ingress would be allowed. So why didn't he try this on the night of 31 August?

Another mystery.

Richard, feeling tensely beleaguered, stepped over two trails of drying urine and went to sit on a wooden bench on the path opposite Harry's. On the ground there were flattened cigarette packets with the health warnings in Polish. The lads had left him out here on his own. *Laura* had left him out here on his own. There was a hard clot of outrage in the centre of his chest. He kicked at one of the cigarette packets. He took out his mobile and rang Stephen O'Brien, who didn't answer.

Inside Laura said, 'Poor Richard. Someone should go out to him.'

Laura, too, was very drunk. But she was better at concealing it.

'We'll get a table first,' Stephen O'Brien said. 'Hang on.'

From the dance floor Conor Harris watched as Laura followed Steve across the bar.

Richard stewed on the bench outside for half an hour. His friends had betrayed him: of that much he was certain. He expected it from Foxer and O'Brien but what the *fuck* did Laura think she was doing? *He* would never have gone inside without *her*. A painful throbbing began in Richard's left temple. His complacency had rudely deserted him. The most beautiful girl in the club was his, of course; but she had gone inside without him. Richard felt a pang of the purest jealousy. For all he knew Laura could already have her tongue stuck halfway down the throat of some cunt from Merrion Academy.

He dialled Laura's number. But inside the club the music was too loud for anyone to hear their mobile phone.

At 11.00 pm Stephen O'Brien brought a trayful of tequila slammers to the table that the Dalkey gang had found. Everyone knocked one back. They licked the salt and bit the wedge of lemon.

Laura went to the bathroom to reapply her lipgloss. In the cubicle she took her daily dose of Lexapro. You weren't supposed to drink while you were taking Lexapro but Laura had flaunted this rule often enough to know that she would probably be alright.

Out on the seething dance floor, Stephen O'Brien looked at his phone and saw that there were seven missed calls, all from Richard's number. He went outside and found Richard sitting on his bench.

'This is fucking ridiculous, Steve-o,' Richard said. 'I mean, what's the fucking story, like?'

In Stephen's opinion (stated at the trial), Richard was not noticeably drunk at this time.

'Keep your knickers on,' Stephen said. 'We'll only stay for a few, alright?'

'I might as well just hit the road, like,' Richard said.

'No, no,' Stephen said. 'Look, I'll fucking smuggle you out some hooch, alright?'

'Send out Laura,' Richard said.

'Will do,' Stephen said.

He went inside and came back fifteen minutes later with a hip flask of cognac concealed in his hoodie. He passed it to Richard.

'Christ, man,' Stephen said, 'Half of St Anne's Sixth Year is in there. It's like fish in a barrel.'

'Fuck off,' Richard said. He drank from the hip flask. 'Where'd you get this?'

'Got it off Whelehan,' Stephen said. 'He never leaves home without it.'

'Where's Laura?'

'Dunno, man. I'll send her out, yeah?'

Stephen O'Brien went back into Harry's. Richard sat on his bench, drinking from Dave Whelehan's hip flask. He began to smoke some cigarettes of Laura's that he had found in his jacket pocket.

At 11.50 pm Clodagh Finnegan limped over to Stephen O'Brien, complaining that some bitch wearing stiletto heels had accidentally stood on her big toe. Gallantly Stephen knelt to kiss the big toe better. Then he and Clodagh went outside for a smoke. For five minutes or so they kept Richard Culhane company.

By now Richard had, in the words of the prosecution, 'become aggressive'. He shouted at Stephen for not finding Laura. The truth was that Stephen kept forgetting about Richard and Laura. In his own words, he was by this time 'fairly stocious'. He too became aggressive. He told Richard to fuck off and brought Clodagh back inside.

At 12.02 pm Fergal Morrison left Harry's and took Joanna Carruthers home in a taxi.

At 1.04 am Lisa McKeown complained of feeling sick and called her father, who arrived to take her home twenty minutes later.

Conor was now alone in the club.

This is where accounts start to break down. By one o'clock in the morning, everyone was drunk or stoned or scoring. Or they were otherwise engaged – with drug deals, with rivalries, with getting home safe. People's recollections about this part of the night tend to lack clarity. They tend to contradict one another. We know so little. Even after a garda investigation and a trial, even after exhaustive conversations, we know so very little about the things that happened next.

For example: where was Conor and what was he doing between the hours of one and three in the morning? He didn't leave the club. But no one remembers talking to him – or no one admits to remembering, which amounts to the same thing. One theory is that he talked to Laura, but Laura herself maintains that she didn't even know Conor was in the club until he found her at the exit as the crowd trickled out.

I am left with another mystery. If I had been there, perhaps … But I was not.

At 2.30 am the nightclub lights came on and everyone groaned at how pale and tired they looked in the sudden glare. People started queuing for their coats. The bouncers started their cacophonous hustling: 'Move it there, folks, now, *please*, time to *go*.'

Time to go.

Questions (always questions): Why didn't Laura go outside to talk to Richard? Laura herself could never satisfactorily explain this. She was distracted, she said. She was socializing. She was swallowed by the crowd. So why did Richard wait? Why did he sit outside Harry's for almost four hours, waiting for the club to empty? I know the answer to this question. He was waiting for Laura. He sat and sipped with the same stoical fixity he brought to a solitary session on the rugby pitch. It was in his nature.

At around 2.25 am Barry Fox had come outside to wait with Richard. This was in *his* nature. By now the hip flask was empty, but Barry had bought a shoulder of vodka earlier that day and now the two of them finished it off.

At 3.05 am Laura made it to the door of the club. She had been separated from Clodagh and Steve in the crush. She stood outside the door and looked around for Richard, but the crowd obscured her view.

Laura hugged herself and felt the grain of gooseflesh on her arms. She took the star-spangled hoodie from her bag and put it on.

This was how girls looked at the end of a night out: the glamourous dress half-covered by the homely hoodie.

Outside the nightclub there were girls who had taken off their painful shoes and now stood in bare feet on the edge of the path, signalling for oblivious taxis. Each of the barefoot girls was squired by a teetering young man in a rugby jersey.

At 3.07 am Conor Harris emerged from Harry's and saw Laura Haines standing by herself.

By now Conor was feeling rakish, and pleasurably drunk. He imagined, I think, that Laura would welcome him in a spirit of camaraderie. He did not, as some people have asserted, 'leer' at Laura, nor did he say anything 'inappropriate'.

Of course, when he said hello to Laura at the door, the time when Conor's actions made a difference to his fate had already come and gone.

'Nice hoodie,' Conor said.

'Thank you,' Laura said.

'You're welcome,' Conor said.

Then they spotted Richard, weaving towards them from the other side of the street. When Laura looked for Conor, she found he had disappeared.

'Were you talking to that fucker?' Richard said.

'He just said hi, Richard.'

'Come on,' Richard said, putting his arm around Laura's neck. 'Let's get the fuck out of here.'

'*Relax*, Richard,' Laura said.

Richard stopped, and leaned away from her, scanning her body with a critical eye.

'Nice hoodie,' he said. 'What the fuck did you wear that for?'

'I was cold,' Laura said.

'I'm fucking going home,' Richard said. He strode off, shaking his head and swearing at the sky.

They were a little way along the main street now, away from the majority of the people who had spilled out of the club. But the street was still crowded, still full of barefoot girls and teetering boys. Laura followed Richard. She shouted his name.

It was 3.15 am.

And Conor Harris found Richard Culhane in the crowd.

We don't know who said what. We don't know who did what. After all this time, we still don't even know who threw the first punch. Richard said it was Conor. Other people said it was Richard. Still other people said it was Stephen O'Brien.

But it doesn't matter.

The first punch got thrown and then all of them were on him. Stephen and Barry had been a step behind Richard. They were there when it mattered. Conor flailed out with his stocky arms but there were too many people. There were six to ten people and Conor could do nothing.

Afterward Richard remembered only the hatred. He wanted to hurt his own body in the cause of damaging Conor's. He wanted the exhilaration of it. He wanted the pain.

What did they do to him?

They punched at his belly and ribs for a while, until they got bored of that and moved on to his face. Someone got him in the kidneys – both sides. Stephen O'Brien worked at tripping him, hacking away at his legs.

They punched his face. They elbowed his face. They squeezed his arms and the hollows of his neck. This was a drunken fight. There was no precision. They fought with each other to get a clear punch at Conor. Most of the time they didn't even know what they were hitting. They lashed out and waited for the sound of yielding flesh.

There was already a lot of blood on Conor's face. Bruises had closed his eyes. No one remembered him speaking. He may not have made a sound.

He was still standing at this point. Barry Fox dug his fist into Conor's sternum, then pulled his arm back and landed a punch so heavy it caused his knuckles to ache for days.

(So that all through the next day, as he sat in Pat Kilroy's office, as he wrote his statement and met his girlfriend, Barry was nursing his sore right hand.)

Laura staggered backwards into Mick Conroy's idling taxi. She was shouting at the boys to stop.

Richard drove his forearm into Conor's nose. He felt the snap of breaking bone. He said, '*Fuck you*,' without recognizing his own voice.

Conor looked like he was asleep. The press of the crowd had kept him upright, but now a gap had formed. And he fell.

The back of his head struck the concrete of the path.

Richard felt Conor's fall as a kind of consummation. He remembered the intimacy of fighting, the need to be close to another human body, like lovemaking but with the opposite intention: the intention to cause harm, the intention to silence, the intention to punish.

Conor, dying, fell to the ground and did not get up.

One witness remembered seeing a young man rush into the melee at this point and deliver a swinging kick to Conor's chest. Then he ran away. This young man has never been identified.

Laura was shouting. She had started to cry. People were running away. By now only three boys were near enough to do Conor any damage.

Bang.

Was it Stephen O'Brien who took the first running kick, as though aiming for the conversion in a Senior Cup final?

Bang.

The second kick – I can say with reasonable confidence – was Barry Fox's. He admitted as much during his first interrogation.

Bang.

Was this Richard? Was it? Believe it if you want. It's up to you.

'This can't be happening,' Laura said. 'This can't be happening.'

Time seemed to gulp down an obstruction and resume its normal pace.

It was 3.16 am.

'Oh, you think you're such a big man,' Laura said to Richard Culhane.

'Christ,' said Barry Fox. 'I think we should call an ambulance. Guys, I fucking think we should call an ambulance.'

'We fucking showed that little cunt,' said Stephen O'Brien.

55

I seem to have gotten bigger, since Conor died. I don't mean that I've put on weight. I mean I feel bulkier, more physically formidable, as though there is now a great deal more of me to carry around. And, of course, there is: now I carry Conor, too, who cannot carry himself. Brother, you were so big, and you left so much behind. My spirit sags with all your heft. There is so much I have to haul out of bed every morning, so much excess baggage. And things matter more to me, or seem to. Grief is supposed to make things matter less, but now I seem so raw, I feel things so acutely – raindrops, windshear, hunger, thirst – that every small sensation seems to kick me in the guts. A heavy spirit incurs heavy damage. But my damage is no match for yours, not yet. Until I go to Inishfall I will be an amateur of pain. And you were the professional, of course, the deft absorber of all those shocks. In your last three hours you condensed a lifetime of suffering – almost neatly, it seems to me now, with hardly any waste or fuss.

Goodbye, brother. Sorry I couldn't do more.

56

Conor lay on the tarmac for almost two hours, sporadically attended by friends and passers-by. He was still breathing. His throat made a pulpy sound as he inhaled. After that wait – that terrible, terminal two-hour wait – the fluorescent men in their screaming ambulance brought Conor to the hospital, and he died. For half an hour – no more – the plastic clothes peg of the heart monitor was clamped over his right index finger. The doctors and nurses looked at his face and head and realized that they were probably dealing with massive internal bruises, and possibly a fractured skull. Conor's airway was partially obstructed – all this is from the emergency room report, cited in several papers. They pumped him full of adrenaline and they intubated him. They scheduled an MRI for noon. But Conor didn't last that long.

There had already been an incident of cardiac arrhythmia in the ambulance. The paramedics had shocked him with the paddles, and he had rallied. A shaky optimism prevailed, for a while. But. But. But.

It wasn't Eileen Harris or Brendan Harris who identified Conor's body. They found they weren't able. Conor's brother had to do it.

I had to do it.

They had him in a basement room, laid out on a trolley with the sidebars folded down. My baby brother, I thought. Because they never stop being babies, do they? Younger siblings, I mean. They're babies to someone till the day they die. And that someone, in Conor's case, was me. After our parents were gone, I would have still been around to look after him. I would still have been, in some sense or other, in loco parentis. But now it wasn't going to work that way.

The room was cold, of course. They refrigerate the dead, to stop them rotting. There was the chilly, disinfected smell of hospitals, a seminal thickness in the settled air. I stood beside the trolley and said, 'Yes, that's him. That's my brother.'

'Conor?' said the nurse with the clipboard, and made a note.

I nodded. I felt very capable, very cool. I looked at Conor's head and seemed to see a small concavity, a bluish dent above the closed right eye. He looked handsome in the blank luminescence.

Then I went outside and told my parents that the boy on the trolley was Conor and that he was dead.

For several months I didn't sleep. Instead there was a kind of waking coma, a visionary trance in which I saw repeated over and over the same silent drama: Conor, dying. I didn't really talk to my parents, which I know caused them still greater anxiety and pain. I went to the funeral and I went to the trial and I told Father Connelly to fuck off when he called to our door, but during all of this I was a ghost, as much of a ghost as Richard seemed to be, mouthing the usual pleases and thank yous but absent, really, hopelessly involved in some prior trauma, so that everything I did seemed belated, superfluous, even cruel – cruel to Conor, I mean, who could no longer do even the simplest thing.

Eventually I came partway back, and told my parents to take the holiday in Kinsale. I thought it might do them good to get away from a house which had been so palpably diminished in scope and integrity by Conor's loss. While they were gone I sat in Conor's room – now a guestroom, and efficiently anonymous. I sat on Conor's bed (the same bed, the bed he had slept in and masturbated in and perhaps even fucked Laura Haines in) and tried to understand what had happened.

I haven't – it will have become clear – been entirely honest in preparing this account. I've left myself out, because I had to. But I was there all along, for a great deal of the incidental stuff. Where the inconsequential sections are concerned, I can vouch for the truth of what I say. I can vouch for what Laura Haines looked like as she ate an apple outside Simmonscourt Pavilion in May of 2003. I can vouch for what Pat Kilroy said at Conor's funeral. I can vouch for what Conor looked like in the morgue.

I was there for so much. I was there, awkwardly loitering, in Conor's bedroom when he cried himself to sleep because Laura Haines had broken up with him. I was there, shouting from the sidelines with self-conscious abandon, for every Senior Cup match Conor played. I was there when he trained and I was there when they left him on the bench. He seemed to expect this kind of loyalty, and I was glad to give it to him. But I wasn't – I couldn't have been – there when he lay bleeding on the ground, waiting for an occupied ambulance. And this is why I can't tell this story, not properly, not completely. This is why so much of what I have to say is merely guesswork. It's because I wasn't there when my baby brother died.

I wasn't there.

I've tried to be as scrupulously accurate as possible in reconstructing these events. Grief is a scrupulously accurate emotion. It gives us a thirst for the precise. I used my sorrow, too, to get people to talk. I have a kind of gravity, now. People give me leeway. They indulge my rambling theories.

I owe the most, perhaps, to Laura Haines.

Laura was my source for much of this – for the stuff I wasn't present for myself. She was my chief source of information about Richard and his family. For a while we met in UCD, where Laura was now studying Business in the Quinn School. (Her nursing degree, in the aftermath of Conor's death, had come to seem like an unfeasible proposition.) We had lunch in the Quinn School café, where Richard and Conor had lounged with their laptops and their competing entourages of rouged and bouffant girls. The place was full of the usual people – boys in cords and rugby tops, girls in denim skirts and ursine boots. I looked around at them: the boys and girls, laughing and flirting, carrying on as though everything was still the same. They were all much younger than me, of course. Laura's was the only face I recognized.

For an hour or so we would talk about what had happened. I asked because I needed to know, and Laura told me because she needed to tell. It was a way of feeling closer to Conor, sitting opposite this girl that he had loved. But it was also a way of feeling closer to someone else. It was a way of feeling closer to Richard Culhane.

We both need Laura, Richard and I, and for the same reason: she is our final link to Conor Harris. She knows this, and she is generous with her time. But this cannot last forever. I will meet her for one last lunch, but after that we will all be on our own.

I have very little left to say. Now that my story is almost told I am too full, not of words but of their opposites: silence, absence, loss.

Conor, I tried my best to keep you safe. I tried to do what an older brother should. But I couldn't help you. I wasn't there.

No more of that.

I will go to Inishfall. But not yet, not yet. Not until my work is done. When there is no more left to do, I will follow the Culhanes to their fallen island. I will go to Inishfall.

57

It was almost winter when the Culhanes set out for Inishfall. There was chimney smoke in the darkening air, the weather was getting colder, the evening was falling earlier and earlier as they tidied up the house in Sandycove and got themselves ready for the journey westward.

Time to go.

They knew they had to get away. One Tuesday in October Richard, anxious for the flavour of his previous life, had borrowed Peter's car (they had sold Richard's Nissan to pay for legal costs) and driven up to UCD. The café in the Quinn School was full of people he recognized. They sat at their tables with their laptops and their €3 coffees and they looked at all the places where Richard wasn't standing. Richard sat at an empty table near the window and drank an espresso. He had ordered an espresso because he knew it was the thing he could drink the quickest.

Barry Fox was wiser: when his prison term was over he enrolled at the University of Manchester and is now studying for a degree in Social Policy.

Of the three Harry's Niteclub boys, Stephen O'Brien proved to be the most successful at re-establishing a kind of southside life. He insisted, as loudly and as often as he could, that of the three boys convicted, his role in the fight had been the smallest, the least significant. I don't think Richard or Barry blamed him for this. They understood what he was trying to do. Nowadays I think Steve studies Business at one of the Dublin technical colleges.

Peter and Katherine Culhane knew they had to leave because they no longer had anyone to talk to who wasn't Gerald Clinch or Namwali or their only son. For a short time Father Connelly had continued to call to the Sandycove house, but when the manslaughter trial collapsed even his patronage rapidly ceased.

Peter had become aware that he and Richard rarely spoke and never touched. They had never been particularly affectionate, but now Peter sharply missed the unimprovable gratification of being hugged by his child. He watched his wife and son drift around the house and realized they needed to be somewhere else.

So it was Peter who made the decision. 'Why don't we go to Inishfall for a couple of weeks?' Richard and Katherine agreed. They were both aware – or they both suspected – that the family would stay in the big white house on the island for longer than a couple of weeks. They wondered if Peter felt this way. He had become, in the aftermath of the trial, inscrutably polite, attentive to irrelevant nuances of politesse and good behaviour. He helped Richard pack his bags, insisting that they take with them Richard's rugby boots. Richard waited until Peter had left the room and unpacked the boots. He knew he wouldn't need them.

So the family left for Inishfall, taking with them everything they meant to us. Katherine had to tell Namwali that her services would no longer be required. She cried as she did it. Namwali's final paycheck was accompanied by a substantial bonus. The women, in tears, embraced and wished each other luck. When Namwali had gone Katherine was consumed by self-pity. Was this how bad she had become, that she sought comfort in the arms of a black woman, a woman to whom none of her friends would even speak?

Eventually they had been on the island for so long that Peter told Gerald Clinch to arrange for the Sandycove house to be rented out. I think an American family lives there now. Clinch had asked for surprisingly little money, because he knew he was offering tainted goods.

Two weeks after the Culhanes departed in their overloaded car for Inishfall, Laura Haines ran into Elaine Ross and Rebecca Dowling outside Karen Millen on Grafton Street. They chatted for five minutes about their Ailesbury College days. To Laura this felt like talking about a book she had read a long time before. Then they went to the Avoca Café for coffee.

Elaine asked Laura what visiting Richard in prison had been like.

'Depressing,' Laura said.

'He must have been, like, *so* grateful,' Elaine said.

Laura said nothing.

Rebecca said, 'Did you see they have a sale on in Topshop?'

Elaine said, 'I mean, I heard even his *parents* wouldn't visit him.'

'Where did you hear that?' Laura said tonelessly.

'I just heard it,' Elaine said. 'You know Naomi Frears is going out with Kevin Kerrigan now? How weird is that?'

'She spoke at the funeral,' Laura said.

'Oh yeah,' Elaine said.

There was a silence. Then Elaine said, 'And have you seen him recently, like? Richard, I mean. I mean I wonder how he is.'

'He's down on Inishfall,' Laura said. 'I'm supposed to go and see him soon.'

'Oh,' Elaine said. 'Well listen, good luck, alright? Tell him we were asking for him, like.'

The girls embraced and said goodbye.

That weekend Laura caught the InterCity Express to Kerry. It was early on the Saturday morning and the train was almost empty. From the window of her carriage, somewhere past Kildare, Laura saw a rugby pitch. Under the thin, raked shadow of the posts she could make out a long white sweep of speckled frost.

Peter Culhane met her at the station and drove her out to Inishfall. As they crossed the concrete bridge the tide was in and the beaches of the island were invisible beneath the inundating sea. Laura looked at Peter as he drove. He was badly shaven – as though he had let someone do it for him instead of doing it himself – but his eyes were bright and clear. He drove with his hands reassuringly loose on the steering wheel. Laura knew she was looking at the last remnants of Peter's patrician competence. By force of habit he was still an erratically charming man. But he didn't speak to her until they arrived at the house.

'Your room's at the top of the stairs on the left,' he said, and went inside carrying her sports bag.

Laura also knew that Peter and Katherine feared her visit. She was the last connection the Culhanes possessed to the events that had destroyed their comfort and renown. It was Richard who had invited her to the island. She knew she could expect no welcome from his parents.

The house was emptier than Laura had expected. The rooms had an air of neglect, as though the house had just been opened at the beginning of the summer. She waited, alone in the kitchen, for Richard to come down.

He looked like his old self when he arrived: the gelled hair, the Ben Sherman shirt, the crisply ironed cords. He was neatly shaven, too, and handsome – handsome as he had never been when Laura went to visit him in prison.

'Hey,' he said.

'Hey,' Laura said.

Peter and Katherine bustled into the kitchen. Katherine kissed Laura and asked how she was getting on in college. Peter put the kettle on.

A needling rain began to fall.

Peter served tea and they sat around the kitchen table, looking out at the stormy afternoon light.

Nobody knew what to say.

Eventually Richard asked Laura to come upstairs with him. They went into Richard's room. He had not unpacked, and his suitcase lay under a pile of unwashed clothes.

Peter and Katherine sat in the conservatory. Katherine mixed them drinks, which they didn't touch. They listened for sounds from the room upstairs but they heard nothing.

Richard and Laura were up there for an hour. I don't know what they said. Laura wouldn't tell me. And I know she never will.

This is the last lacuna in my story, the last event about which I can have no certain knowledge. What did Richard say to Laura? What did Laura say to Richard? I have no answers. Once again: I have no answers.

After an hour in Richard's room Laura came downstairs. She was crying. Katherine and Peter stood in the kitchen while Laura sat at the table and cried. The silence went on and Richard did not come down. When a roll of thunder rumbled in the sky above the bay, the three people in the unlit country kitchen half-awoke, as from a dream of judgment.

Looking suddenly haggard, Peter touched Laura's shoulder and said, 'I'll drive you back to the station.'

And so Laura fetched her bag and threw it in the boot of Peter's car. They drove past low stone walls the colour of iron, past fields of sharp grass that grew from damp, sandy soil. The sky was low and troubled and the air was full of something cold. Peter dropped Laura at the station in Tralee.

'Goodbye,' he said.

'Goodbye, Peter,' Laura said.

They shook hands, and Peter drove away.

Time to go.

We are left with so many gaps, so many ambiguities, so many explanations left unfinished. We returned to our careers, of course – I am speaking now of myself and my parents, of Eileen and Brendan Harris and their last remaining son. We went back to work and college and we asked no more of the public world, having been refused so much for so long. Laura went back to university. The others – all those people I have touched on, all those people so crucial to my story, so fruitful of confusion and distress – resumed the running of the country or the running of their lives. They continued. They got on with it.

And the Culhanes?

The Culhanes are receding from us, slowly, year by year. Soon we will have lost them altogether. I think about them often, out there in the west, in the stuffy rooms of their enormous house, waiting in silence as the evenings draw in and the weather gets gradually worse. They are alone on a bleak and emptying island, receding and alone, alone at last where everything ends, sitting out their ruined lives on Inishfall.

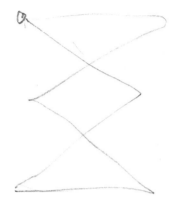